HOME ~~sweet~~ HOME

Desirae Moten

To the teachers, advisors, peers, loved ones, friends, professors, and coworkers in and throughout my life that always encouraged me to write.

14 years later, this book is complete.

ALSO BY DESIRAE MOTEN

Stay-at-Home Calls for Poetry

TABLE OF CONTENTS

Chapter 1: Harvey
1983 - FALL

It's Ma's raised voice that wakes me up at 2 a.m. It's annoying enough they send me to bed at 11. I'm fourteen, I should be able to stay up 'til midnight anyway. Especially if they wake me up hours later.

I walk barefoot, to the top of our wood steps, blending into the shadows underneath Dad's picture of Jimi Hendrix on the wall. He said Hendrix's guitar got him through any funk. It doesn't seem to be working now.

I can't see my parents, but I hear them.

"I didn't spend his money on alcohol. You're not putting that on me," Dad yells at Ma.

"You're not putting this on me. I gave you that money. I told you to get your son a gift," Ma argues.

"What he need more stuff for? He's got a bike and games. We got books in the house he ain't reading. He needs to worry about what he's got here instead of going over other people's houses."

"There's the truth. There it is. You're being cheap."

"How cheap can I be when I'm giving him a roof, food, clothes—"

Ma cuts him off. "*We*. That ain't all you. Don't you dare say it's all you. You got some nerve." Her words are coming out faster. "Everybody pulls their weight in this house. As the parents, you and I work. I also cook—"

"—and what weight do those boys bring?" he interjects. His voice always sounds like he needs to spit. Runners do it all the time, but my dad was never a runner.

"Tim helps me cook and fold the clothes. Harvey cleans around the house."

My dad scoffs. "That ticking bomb. He cleans out of punishment."

I frown. He only punishes me because I keep getting praised in school and he thinks I'm school smart and not street smart. My body doesn't have enough muscle for him. He thinks I can't defend myself in the streets and that he's raising weak men. So, he punishes me and my brother with tedious things to do at home.

"The point is the rules still apply with gifts. There is no from both of us. You pull your weight to show your love," Ma says.

"All I'm saying is we got him a cake, we're throwing a little party, and"—a snarky chuckle escapes him— "we are cooking for family. Nobody got time for more things in this house."

"Nobody got time for more alcohol in this house. All that liquor in your system is changing you."

"I'm fine. I can unwind with something to drink. It ain't a crime."

"Your boys are noticing."

"Noticing what!"

Ma goes silent. I hear a crackling sound. He must be pouring himself more alcohol. His go-to's are rye or bourbon. "That you're not happy," Ma softly says.

That's when I feel a tickle against my arm. I turn to see my brother, Timothy, is awake. "Hey, Tim," I whisper.

"Are they okay?"

I bite my lip and sigh. It's not often he wakes up during their fights. "I don't know."

My brother yawns. He's wearing my old green checkered pajamas. His hair is usually tangly, but because Ma made him get a haircut yesterday, his hair is cut low, no detangling to do. He has white specks around his mouth. Drool still showing up on his brown skin.

"Try to go back to sleep. You got a big day tomorrow."

Tim gets giddy, with a dorky grin, causing his eyes to squint. "Yes, I do."

I put my arm around his shoulders and take a few steps back, so Tim isn't too loud. "I can't believe you're gonna be eleven. Getting older but still looking like a shrimp."

Tim chuckles but elbows my side. "You're the one in high school. Nerd."

I softly laugh at that.

"Can you come back with me?" Tim asks.

I swallow. Tim and I have a shared bedroom. I wanted to hear how our parents would settle the argument, but my brother usually falls back to sleep easily when I'm there. I think me not being in the bed makes him worry about them. "Yeah, Tim." I place both my hands on his shoulders and turn him to our room. "Let's get back to sleep."

The next morning at 7:30, I get up before Tim wakes up. I head in the kitchen to find Ma making chocolate chip pancakes. The only time she gives us chocolate for breakfast is for someone's birthday.

"Hi, Ma."

She turns, and I'm able to see her face. She got her hair done, too, yesterday. She likes to straighten it, then have Ms. Jasmine give her loose curls. She loves the style and the shape of her hair this way. Ear length. "You're awake early," she says.

"I'm going over Lee's real quick. He's giving me something for Tim."

She pauses. "Lee's giving him a gift? That's nice."

"Not exactly. It's for me. You'll see when he opens his gifts."

"Okay. Bring his mom's plastic containers back, in the corner over there."

"Okay." I grab them from near the sink before walking three blocks to Lee's house. When I ring the bell Lee's mom answers. "Hi, Ms. Walters."

"What brings you here, Harvey? Lee ain't even awake yet."

"Ma said to bring you your plastic containers. And I can wake up Lee. I just need his help real quick."

Ms. Walters takes them from me as I walk in the house. "Alright. Thank you. I think he was up all night with that Atari. His uncle was doing the most getting him that Frogger game." She closes the door.

I chuckle. "It's a pretty good gift."

"It's your brother's birthday today, right?"

"Yeah."

"We got him a card somewhere. Lee kept forgetting to bring it when he'd go over your house." She looks in the living room. "Where did we leave it?"

"While you look for that I'll be back." I jog up their unsqueaky steps. Lee's mom got the first floor remodeled after Lee cut open his arm from the mantel in the house. After that she started noticing every problem on the first floor and got it done, including their older staircase. It definitely looks more '80s than '60s now.

I open Lee's bedroom door. Lee has his green covers over his head, feet sticking out the bottom. I walk over to his bed and smack his back twice. "Wake up, Lee." I shake what I think is his shoulder and arm. "Lee."

Lee uncovers his face and blinks in confusion. "Whoa. Gosh."

"Hey."

Lee rubs his eyes before yawning his question, "What are you doing here?"

I sit in his desk chair and use my feet to spin slightly back and forth. "My dad's not giving Tim a gift."

"Again?"

I'm used to not getting gifts from dad; I don't want Tim to be. "My mom doesn't believe in teamed up anything. I remember when I was nine, I made a card and had Tim write his name at the bottom with mine. She was upset I didn't encourage Tim to make his own card. She said I could have helped him with the spelling." I shake my head.

"You woke me up for this?"

"My point, can I have your Etch A Sketch?"

He yawns, mouth wide. I imagine the invisible fog being a stink bubble released in the air. Luckily, I'm far enough away to not smell it. It pops on his door. "Why?"

"I saved up. I can get you another one. For today, can I please just wrap yours?"

Lee scratches his head, his twists in all directions. He props himself up with his arm. "You owe me."

"Yes." I nod and clap my hands together. "Serious. I got you."

"It's under those papers and boxes." Lee points to his desk behind me.

I turn and move the boxes, careful not to knock over his slinky, to get it. Lee and I have opposite desks. He has cluttered boxes from games he's opened, and I have notebooks for my writing.

"What's Tim gonna say about it not being in the box?"

I shrug. "I wanted to make sure it actually worked. No mess ups or whatever."

He chuckles and lays back down. "Whatever. Tell him I say happy birthday."

"You know I'm saying this is from me, not you, right?"

"Yes, dummy." He throws the covers back over his face.

"Thanks, Lee."

. . .

After taking Tim and two of his friends to see a movie in the afternoon, we're spending the evening with family. Mom made chicken parmesan, and because dad thinks he's the only one that knows how to make good mashed potatoes with his special gravy, he made it to complete the meal.

After dinner Tim unwraps his gifts, sitting crisscross on the floor. Three gifts are opened, and two unopened gifts are left. He tears off the green paper from my gift. Tim smiles. "Oh, that's cool. An Etch A Sketch. Thanks Harvey."

I smile. "Just thought we ought to have it in our house too." I'm sitting on the floor but feel Ma's stare on the right side of my head. I turn to see her giving me a questionable look. I nod, still smiling.

Tim grabs a present with white and green wrapping paper. "From Dad," he reads from the handwritten "to-and-from" note that I put on there. He looks at Dad sitting in his special brown chair. "Oooh, oooh."

Ma's eyes get small, and her brows tense, exchanging glances in Dad and my directions.

Dad shrugs at Ma. His hairless face allows me to see every unamused wrinkle. He looks back at Tim, his head tilted in slight confusion. "Well, open it," he grunts.

Ma looks at me again. "What is that?" she mouths.

I ignore her.

Tim opens it to find a Walkman and two cassettes. "No way! No way!" he stands up. "Yes. Thanks, Dad."

Uncle Roger, Grandma, and Uncle L laugh at Tim's excitement.

Ma's lips pout, and I know I'm in trouble.

I look past her, at Dad's reaction. Dad is shaking his head. I know it's because he thinks it's another expensive piece of junk in the house. "Tim, what's the cassettes?" I ask.

Tim goes back and looks. "Whoa, Journey? And Stevie! This is the best!"

"Mm, it's too much," Dad says.

Tim smiles wide. "You still gave it to me."

Dad flags his hand. His squinty eyes turn to the window as he rubs his beer belly, though that's the only alcohol he doesn't drink.

If dad doesn't like it, but Tim does, it means it's a good gift. I know how to make my brother happy. "Now Stevie Wonder can sing happy birthday to you directly."

"He's gonna be absorbed in that all day," grandma says.

"That's a gift you and your brother take turns with," Ma tells Tim. "Harvey, help me get the cake." Ma stands up, not looking at me. She goes into the kitchen. "Now," echoes behind her.

I sigh, getting up off the floor, and follow.

Ma takes the cake out of the fridge and puts it on the counter and then places a hand on her hip. "Why on earth did you say that gift was from your father?"

"Because he didn't get Tim anything."

"And your father should live with being that cruel to his sons."

"I'm used to it; Tim shouldn't be. I didn't want him feeling some type of way toward Dad."

Ma gets closer to me, her eyes sad, and places her hands on the sides of my face. "You saved for that Walkman." I look down. "You're a good brother."

"You're a good mom."

She makes a psh sound and let's go of me. She turns to Tim's vanilla cake. The words 'Happy Birthday, Tim' are written so professional it makes me wonder if Ma got this from a store or a fancy cake place. "I'm trying."

I don't get why Dad and Ma are still together. They either have fights like they did last night or just talk about money. They don't really seem happy. Are they staying together for Tim and me? Or maybe it's just for Tim.

Dad doesn't want to get to know me. He judges my interest in writing, judges my excitement for school and learning.

She picks up the cake. "Grab the plates and forks."

"Would you leave Dad?" blurts out my mouth.

She turns to me and shakes her head. "Not for not getting y'all presents."

"You said you don't like him drinking."

Her mouth slants to the side and she lowers her eyes. "He's just going through a rough patch. He found out some news that made him upset." She extends her pointer finger at the drawer near the sink, careful not to drop the cake. "Grab a knife too."

What news? Did someone die? Did he get in a fight with someone? But she walks back into the living room while the lemon sweet icing scent stays lingering in the air.

Chapter 2: Lasher
2011 - WINTER

I pace our apartment. I already cleaned the kitchen and the bathroom for a second time today. I don't know what else to do. Dad hasn't texted me an update since last night. Whatever's going on, it feels really bad this time. Like he's dug himself into a deeper hole. It has to be about money. It always is with him.

I go to my room and search each of my stash spots for a fourth time. Nothing in my socks. Only a penny in my marble jar. Nothing in the backpack of my stupid toy figurine of a boy, with a piercing smile, wearing jeans, and a striped shirt that makes him look like a killer. I always keep him faced down, that's how I know my dad took money from him. He was facing up on my windowsill, and only one out of the two zippers were zipped up on his backpack. I try to remember if I have any other money stored that he hasn't found yet. That could possibly help. I remember under my bed, three shoe boxes back against the wall, I keep a photo album. And in a little slot in the back of the photo album, I slid a fifty dollar bill.

I get on my stomach and lay across the carpet, reaching underneath my bed. One box, two boxes… I stretch out my arm, until I feel the third box. Just like I remembered. I slide the box out and toss the lid off. I sit up and flip to the end of the book. I'm not in the mood to look at my childhood or get stuck wondering why I kept that one picture of my mom.

I don't even look happy in the picture. She clearly wanted to take it, and I wanted to do something else. She's basically forcing me beside her so I can be in the picture. The dumb part is, her smile is real. She's actually convincing herself she's happy. I didn't hide my annoyance then, like I do now. I wonder what it felt like to be that kid. To just embrace emotions and care only about my needs and wants.

I slip my hand in the slot and the fifty dollar bill is still there. Dad didn't know about this hiding spot. What was his plan? The sad part is I know his goal. My dad just wants me back in school. He wants to feel like he's not messing up, especially when I only have three years left before I'm a part of the graduating class of 2013. He wants to be an adult the right way. He isn't though. He's a mess.

A fucking mess.

Who loses two jobs and a house and blames their son? He does.

Who gets stuck in a first floor apartment near the busy and loud highway and blames their son? He does.

Who gets so angry that they don't get another anger management coach or try an over-the-phone session, but instead, leaves without an explanation? He does.

He's so messed up, he doesn't realize he's blaming me instead of himself. He's full of rage and so am I. He could be a good dad if he let someone help. He's been a good dad before; I don't want him to slip back to old habits now.

Dad used to volunteer at the school and donate whenever they asked as a thank you for me getting an education. He worked at a café in a bookstore and sales over the phone. But he wasn't making his quota.

I sit on my bed and look down. I shake my head. I can't cry. I can't be mad at him. He's trying. I slap my cheek, hitting the cheekbone instead of the squishy part. I let my head turn to the right on impact, but it wasn't that hard of a hit. I know he'll figure this all out. I slap the other side of my cheek for doubting he'll figure it out. This time it's a harder hit.

I let out a breath and look at my wall. A normal teenager's room would have posters or pictures with friends. Maybe even a 2010 calendar or a wall of awards or childhood trophies. I have nothing. A white room. I keep it so clean it's like I'm a guest in this apartment. But, I am a guest in this place. This isn't home. I want our old house.

No. That two floor, no yard, attached to neighbors, old fashion, grandparents-smelling place was never home either. The carpets were dingy, the walls were faded, my room was tiny, my dad's room was big, and he looked so tiny in it. Our living room and kitchen were from a different year. It felt like it was trying to make us something we weren't. It was a roof over our heads and an accomplishment we were proud of. But it still was never right.

Nothing we do feels just right. Something is always off. And I hate to say it's his fault because I could've did more. I could've got another job instead of just babysitting and walking animals. I could've stepped up, so it wasn't all him. He said it himself, I gotta work for my dreams. If I want us to have a better house, I gotta do my part.

I stand up. Tears are forming in my eyes, but I can't let them surface. I look at the ceiling, at the walls, at the door, and then at my flip phone on my bed. I check if he called or texted, but still nothing. It's 3:46 p.m. I slide my phone in my pocket and go to the bathroom. Flicking on the light, I go to the mirror. I'm okay. I shake my head, looking at the healing red scar on my brown face. I hear his shouting echoing in my ears.

He didn't mean it. He was so angry he just threw the book. Intended for the air, but it hit me. I was too busy wincing in pain to respond to his question, "Boy, why didn't you move?" I felt him get closer, hovering over me, he yelled in my ear, "Can't you see?" I didn't know the book would smack my face, he did it so fast. When I finally looked at him, he was stunned by the blood above my eyebrow from the book. "Can't you do anything right? You keep fucking up!" He hadn't been that mad in years. I knew in that moment he had to be going through something bad. I wasn't the one fucking up, it was him.

I suggested for us to go back to Virginia. I left out the part of me wanting to go back because it was the place where we figured out things together. We were there for almost seven years. But he was quick to say no. He wanted to handle things himself. He wanted to calm down himself. I dared not suggest anything else.

Like he said, I got in the way. But, he still threw that book in my direction. He could've thrown it anywhere else. And why'd he have to blame me for getting in the way and for this money situation. I don't even get what I did wrong.

A slap crosses my face before I realize I did it to myself. No one else is here. He isn't here. I'm questioning his actions. I'm questioning his love. Fuck, I'm questioning this situation.

Where is he? My other cheek gets slapped, and I straighten up. He will figure it out I tell myself in the mirror through my eyes. He's not abandoning me. He's not giving up. He always figures out a way. That's the one thing about him, he always figures out a way. Dad will end this hurdle.

My phone buzzes and I rip it out my pocket and flip it open.

It isn't him. It's Olivia. My childhood friend. She's asking can she come over because she's upset with her dad. I take a deep breath to not think the same thing. I'm not upset at him. I'm not worried about him. I'm calm. I'm okay. I believe in him.

I text her back that she can come over and then turn on the faucet. I splash my face two times. The cold water feels nice. It awakens and settles me to prepare for Olivia. I can handle a guest. I can be normal. I can listen to her problems and not worry about what's going on in my life. That's what I need right now.

Chapter 3: Harvey
1985 - WINTER

I'm shaken awake in the middle of the night by my grandma. I open my eyes to meet hers, with bags and sagging cheeks. *Why is she still here? I* tried to tell Ma and Dad that I'm sixteen and responsible. I can babysit my brother. But, they said I'm no cook, so Grandma came over.

"There's been an accident," she says.

I pop up. "What do you mean?"

"Your parents are in the hospital." She goes over to Tim. "Timothy, hunny. Tim, get up." She does the same shoulder shake.

Tim turns and then rubs his eyes. "Huh?"

"Tim, we got to go to the hospital," she says.

Tim looks at me, his eyes switching from droopy to panic. We slide on socks and shoes, toss on a jacket, and meet Grandma in the living room. I don't realize I grabbed two different pairs of shoes until we are downstairs. Grandma has on her periwinkle hat, covering her ears, and her black coat. We leave out.

In the car, I demand to know everything. "What happened? Was dad drinking?"

"Calm down, Harvey." She keeps her eyes on the road.

"Are they okay?" Tim asks. He leans between our seats.

"Yes. They both are awake the doctors say." Grandma glances at Tim. "Sit back. Seatbelt on."

Tim slides back and buckles up.

"All I know is that they were in a car accident and alcohol was involved."

My jaw tightens. I shake my head. "He could've killed Ma. He could've killed himself." I slam my hand on the dashboard.

Grandma shakes her head. "Take it easy now. I know he can be reckless, but we don't know the full story."

"They were getting better. He was making Mom happy again," Tim says.

I look at Tim and sigh. He has his arm between his legs and is scratching his forearm through his coat. He does this when he worries about our parents.

When we get to the hospital Ma and Dad are in separate rooms. While Tim and Grandma check on Ma, I look in on Dad. Walking in, I notice a bruise on his head and scratches on his arm. He is watching Johnny Carson.

"You okay?" I manage at the door.

He glances at me and grunts. "I'm in the damn hospital. Can't sleep for another hour 'cause they think I have a concussion." He turns back to the TV. "I wasn't even driving bad. It was that other driver's fault."

I lean on the doorframe. But is that true? He drove drunk before for my birthday. He had forgot to get my cake and I wanted to pick it out. Tim was being watched by Grandma, but Ma and I were in the car. I should've just accepted the ice pops we had in the freezer. But I wanted my cake. All other kids get one, why didn't I? I wanted to be able to tell my friends in school the cool character I chose to be on my cake. It was worth it, until heading back home.

Every time Dad dodged sideswiping a car, sped up on yellow lights, or ignored stop signs, Ma made screeching sounds from the passenger seat. I had thought he was just in a rush to get me back to enjoy my birthday, but she was scared, which made me scared. Ma's sounds told me it wasn't about me at all. Or maybe it was . . .

I wondered why he really did it that night. What was he thinking? Or why wasn't he thinking at all?

"What happened?" I ask.

He looks at me again. "I wasn't drunk driving. I only had a few glasses."

I come off the doorframe in disbelief. He was really fucking drinking. I walk in a circle, silent. He doesn't blame himself at all.

He sits up and throws out his hand. "I was already turning, that driver wasn't paying attention!"

Aren't you supposed to look up to your dad? Or trust him? My mind can't for a second believe him, but I'm not ready to vocalize that to his face.

"You could've been badly hurt! Could've been killed!" I shout, letting worry take over.

"Well, we're still here."

I shake my head and look up at the TV.

"Go on to your mom. I don't even know why you checked on me."

My right hand balls into a fist. "Because I'm not a bad son."

Dad makes a *psh* sound. "I'm the bad guy, right?"

I wasn't going to answer that. Does he not get it's hard to respect him? How can he blame me for being upset? He should be blaming himself. I turn away and walk out.

Across and two doors down to the left is Ma's room. I stand in her doorway as Tim kisses her cheek. Grandma is sitting, not looking at Ma. She is either praying with her eyes open or at a loss for words.

Ma looks worse than Dad. That causes me to ball my fist up again.

Tim turns to me. "How is he?"

I raise one shoulder. "The same. Concussed apparently."

"I'm going to go see him."

"I'm going to the bathroom. Be back." Grandma stands; her footsteps are silent behind Tim's.

I stare at Ma. Her right leg is swollen and suspended in the air. Is she going to be able to walk? Did Dad see her like this? How could he be okay with doing this to her? To them?

"Are you okay?" I move closer to her.

"Uh-hmm."

"Your leg."

"The doctors say I sprained my knee. It'll hopefully heal alright. I gotta take it easy." Her hair is frizzy and matted.

I bring the chair Grandma was sitting in beside Ma's bed and hold her hand. She has a spoon-size bruise along her right arm. "What happened?"

Ma looks at my hand holding hers. I rub it. When she meets my gaze, there are tears in her eyes. "We were having a good time. Everything was going so well. When we got up to leave, that's when I remembered we drove here. I wanted to say something. I knew I should've said something. But I also knew . . . I felt how happy he was. I didn't want him to go off about me talking about us drinking. I said at least he only had two drinks and prayed." Ma shakes her head and looks at the ceiling. "I'm sorry, Lord. I knew it was wrong. Thank you for sparing our lives."

I shake my head and let go of her hand. *Stupid.* They finally got a night out and then he did something like that. Did he really care about their happiness? What about Tim and me?

"Harvey." She turns to me again.

"No, Ma." I stand up. "I can't forgive him for this."

"You will. The Lord forgives me for still stepping in that car. You will forgive me and your dad for doing something so reckless."

I look at the door and lick my lips. "How is it fair that he only walks away with scratches, and you're gonna be walking with a limp?" I look back at her and shout, "That looks bad, Ma!"

"I'm going to be alright. After physical therapy I should be back to wo—"

"Physical therapy? You can't-can't go to work, and he gets to act like everything's normal?"

"We haven't seen each other yet, Harvey. He doesn't know how I'm doing, and I don't know how he's doing."

I shake my head. I want to cover my ears. How is she making excuses for him? How is she still on his side?

"I'm going to be alright," she repeats.

I stare at her. She is trying to convince me to believe her. Her mouth droops to the side, she can't contain her sadness anymore. A tear slides down her cheek.

Her pain doesn't look like it is from her knee, though. It seems it is because of me. My right-hand balls into another fist.

Chapter 4: Lasher
2011 - WINTER

Olivia knocks on the door.

"Hey." I swing open the door.

"Hi. Thanks for having me over." She looks around the living room. "Your dad's not home?"

"No," I respond, facing the door as I close it. I make sure she only sees a glimpse of my left side. The book incident happened four days ago, but the scratch is still healing. The blood made it look worse than it was. Dad helped clean it up, and I only wore a Band-Aid that night and the next day before he left. I think part of him leaving had to do with the Band-Aid since it was a reminder of how bad things were getting. I wanted to prove to him I was fine, but he hasn't come home since.

"Your place is always so neat. It's like a show home or something." I feel her glance at me and then walk toward my room. She glides her hand along the glass bowl near the door.

My dad and I got the bowl at a yard sale we discovered when walking back to our old place from getting cherry water ice's. My dad was looking at some of the books. I thought they were just giving away free candy to people that looked at their yard sale. I took two sweet pops, and my dad took two. The old lady told us to buy the bowl. My dad said no until the lady said, "It always brought my family together. I just kept having something in it. Sometimes chocolate, other times mints, or just candy. Everyone thinks it's just grandma's who have these in their houses, but anyone can."

My dad had picked it up, made a joke about taking the remainder candy and paid $15 for it. In our house it went from candy to change holder to keys holder. But when we moved here, we never kept up with keeping something in it.

I turn and watch Olivia as she goes through my open bedroom door. She takes off her jacket and puts it on my chair, but it immediately falls right to the ground. I vacuumed twice, so it's fine. I'll vacuum again when she leaves. She plops down on my bed in her school uniform: a navy-blue sweater and a dark plaid skirt with, black tights underneath. Her feet hang as she lies back. She stares up at the ceiling.

She knows I don't like anyone sitting on my dad's bed. It's the pullout couch, but we never revert it back to a couch, it's just Dad's bed. And I want it ready for him when he gets back.

I sit beside her, but near the edge of my bed. I stare at my white wall as she tells me about her situation with her dad.

"Yesterday, I suggested to my dad that we bond more. He took it as me trying to bail on school rather than wanting time with him. I go to school all the time. I don't see him all the time," she emphasizes. "But does he listen to that? No. So, I had made a plan with myself to get his attention. And the only things I could come up with are running away to my Aunt Reece or messing up in school where he gets called to come in. I pushed back my Aunt Reece thing because it's close to the holidays, and I want to be with him. I'm getting good grades in my classes, so I basically half-tried with two of my exams. Just two. If I got a D I would still pass."

She continues, "My mind literally wasn't in it anyway." Her fist clenches. "My dad is so irritating with picking up more jobs all the time!"

I listen. Ever since her mom died when she was six, her relationship with her dad has been different. Her dad overworks, fearing they'll end up in the hospital, drown in medical bills, and die like how his wife did. He doesn't make time for Olivia, and it drives her crazy. She wants him home and it sounds like he always runs away from it.

That's actually how we met. We went to grief counseling together. The funny part is, neither of my parents were dead. My mom just lied at the time about my dad dying because I would always cry back then. I had anxiety and stress levels too high for a six year old. I didn't understand back then it was because of how my dad treated my mom. I just remember a lot of yelling in our house.

I thought my mom was taking me to counseling to control my emotions so she'd be able to raise me alone. But, midway through grief counseling, my parents started to date again. I maybe was in counseling for only a year, before we all moved together from Pennsylvania to Virginia. My parents lasted a couple of years. I was probably eight or nine when my mom left. She left me in the relationship. Cared about herself more than her son.

But luckily, that was the push my dad needed to stop being abusive. It's still weird calling it abuse. I don't remember if he ever physically hurt my mom, but he never hurt me. It was all verbal abuse and tension. He got close, but never hurt me. Just emotional stuff.

But when I was like nine, he went to anger management and befriended so many buddies. I remember, because I was surprised to see him happy. I didn't know being with him could feel nice.

I befriended one of the guy's son named Declan. Us and some other kids would be watched by some counselor. Declan's dad was an abusive drunk. Declan and I would talk about our dads or TV shows. He'd always had cool toys he'd let me play with.

Some years after anger management, my dad felt things were going so well that he wanted me to go back to school in Pennsylvania where I started my school years. Freshmen year of high school, I reunited with Olivia. She said I looked the same, just taller. Everything was going great.

Olivia continues, "But, Brother William must've been surprised with how quick I finished compared to others and looked over my exam. The school called my dad, concerned if something was going on with me at home. He got mad at me in the car, saying I was calling him a bad dad and blaming him for my actions. Maybe I was, but I was more trying to tell him I need him. That any other teenager would love to be away from their parents, but I actually want to be around him. I got out the car; he wanted me to get back in. We had a standoff, he drove off to go around the block, and I ran for the bus, so I wouldn't be there when he got back."

I let out a breath. She's in school, her dad can afford to keep her in school and she's failing on purpose. That irks me. But she doesn't know the reason I'm not in school.

Words fly out my mouth. "You're jeopardizing school to prove a point?" I shake my head. "That's not how you go about it. That's dumb. Pass your classes." I try to hit her with logic. "I thought you wanted your dad to hang out with you, not babysit you. You're playing games. Just be honest."

"It's not like you're a perfect student."

"Don't come at me." I know she wouldn't have said it if she knew why I wasn't in school. Kids would love to skip school or miss a year, and I actually want to go back. What type of teenager am I?

"Ugh," she lets out.

I lie down next to her. "Just tell him it feels like you don't even have a dad when you're with him. Tell him the truth."

"I did," she says.

"Are you sure?"

She sits up, and I try to turn over, but it's too late. I know she saw my face finally.

"Lash, what happened?" Her voice is softer.

"Nothing."

"That cut."

I shake my head and sit up. I thought my complexion would be able to hide it, but I guess even on pennies you see the scratches. "Forget about it." I have my back to her again. I pull at my fingers, not wanting to have this talk.

"Are you okay?" she slides forward beside me.

"Fine."

"You're not," she says.

"He's fine." I try to convince her and myself about my dad. I hang my head, shaking it.

"Is this the first time he's hit you?"

"He didn't hit me. This was an accident with a book."

"Lash, is your dad . . .?" She's serious, but keeps a soft tone. She doesn't finish her question. Abusing me? Hitting me? Hurting me? Okay? The answer is "no" to all of them.

I shake my head. He just yells. A few days before the book incident, he was so angry he got in my face, backed me against the wall right outside of my bedroom door. He said, "You see what happens when I try to do it all? Take care of the house, your school, go to work, and be nice all the time!" He bobbled his head back and forth as he listed, "Be nice to the neighbors, your teachers, people at work, the fucking crossing guards." He was referring to before we moved here. "But still this shit happens. We lose it all! And you have the nerve to tell me you can help? You have the nerve to ask me about Massachusetts? Ask me if I want to go home!"

He slammed the wall near my neck. "What home? Home isn't a place! Home is where the people who stand by you are. You gonna leave me?"

I stood up straight and didn't make eye contact with him, because I didn't want to show him fear.

"Answer me," he shouted. So, I stared at a dent on the wall across from me. It had been there since we moved here. I let that be my focus as I shook my head, so he knew I didn't want to leave him. That wasn't what I meant. "I was taught you pull your weight to show your love. I was—" But he cut himself off. The silence lasted thirty seconds longer than I expected, so I turned my head slowly to the right to see his face. But he was turned toward the couch, and I couldn't tell what he was thinking.

"It doesn't matter," I tell Olivia.

"Lasher." She grabs my arm.

"He's just going through stuff right now," I cut her off, moving my arm out of her grip. I stand up. I clench and unclench my hands. My dad is all I have. I don't want her calling Child Protective Services or anyone.

"You know that's not an excuse. Don't stick up for him."

I turn to her. "What am I supposed to do instead?" I get up and pace from my door to the wall, looking at the carpet. "Leave my dad? Everyone abandons him. I'm not going to do that. He's never abandoned me. He cares about me."

"He needs help if he's hurting you."

"He loves me," rushes out my mouth, but my voice cracks. She looks at me with sad eyes.

"I'm not doubting that," she says.

"He's my family." I tell her. The only family I have.

"Then why is he abusing you?" She has her hands intwined but spread open. Looking at me as if I'm helpless and a little kid.

I'm not a little kid. I'm not clueless to what is going on. I just . . . I just don't want to lose the only person in my life because he's going through something. I back against my wall and tears build in my eyes. I press my fist to my forehead. Why does he do this? He makes it so difficult to love him. He is lovable. He just won't let anyone help. He won't listen to me. I'm not just a kid. I'm trying to help. "I can help him," I cry. "He stopped before, he can stop again," I whisper.

But her shoulders sink when I say that. She looks down and then back at me. "Lash…" she doesn't say whatever she wanted to say.

I press the back of my head against the wall and stare at the corner of the ceiling. A tear slides down my cheek. "Don't tell anyone. Please." It will make things worse right now.

When I hear silence, I look at her, and she's biting her lip. She's contemplating. I just want him to come back first and then he can get help. I just want to see him okay. I don't want him to get home and then he's bombarded and arrested.

I get off the wall and brush a tear away. "You didn't come here for me. You came here to get your mind off things. Let's just watch something." I clear my throat and turn to my shelf. I can't let Olivia be involved. She doesn't know my dad; she just thinks she does. "What movie?" I ask. "Let's just be normal, forget our dads and their issues for a moment."

I feel her eyes on me as she says, "Mmm, I-I don't know."

"In the mood for an animated movie, action, comedy?" I swallow.

"Uh, maybe comedy?" She doesn't sound interested.

"Yeah. Yeah, comedy." I glance at her over my shoulder.

She stands up, tugging at her sweater sleeve. "I'm going to go to the bathroom. Surprise me with what you choose." She tucks her twists behind her ear and gives a small smile before walking out my room and turning left to the bathroom.

I find *Dr. Dolittle* and lay it on my dresser. What if she's calling her dad about my dad? What if she's telling someone? I go to the bathroom door, but I don't hear anything. I can't just be a creep at the door.

I should just drink something to ease my mind. That's what I need right now, my soda. I go in the fridge and the last can of orange soda is sitting there. Dad had got me a 12-pack last month. He doesn't drink soda, but he knew this was my favorite and wanted to cheer me up about our money situation. I told myself I wouldn't chug through them all. That I'd drink them sparingly because I knew money was tight. I'm glad I held one for now.

I pull it out of the fridge and open it just as Olivia is coming out the bathroom. I pause, for her to go in my room first. I lift the can to take a sip, but she takes it from me. "Thank you," she says.

"Hey, no." I snatch the soda back.

"Hey. I'm the guest. You should be giving me a drink."

I follow her into my room. Her phone vibrates, and she checks it. She doesn't reply, instead, she tosses her slide on my bed. I hope she didn't tell her dad or anyone. I put the soda on the TV stand. Maybe, I should just tell her all that's going on. I bite my lip. "You kn—" I started, but I'm cut off. There is a loud bang from the front door.

Olivia grasps at my arm, scratching me a little. Her eyes are wide, and mouth tightly closed.

We hear something crash and then, "Dammit." It's not my dad's voice.

"Weapon," I whisper. I pull us both to my closet. She looks at me startled. I push past my coat and a backpack to get to a baseball bat. She blinks, staring at the bat unexpectedly. I inhale and exhale, my body trembling. I'm going to have to do something. Someone's here. If they want my dad, this may not end well. If they're just burglars, that might be better.

We look at my half-opened door, waiting to see a shadow draw near. Olivia stays behind me. Someone approaches my door. I should charge now. I should charge now; I try to convince myself.

I gasp as a white, bald head is peaking its way in my room. I run at him and hit him over the head. The guy backs into the living room, and I follow him, swinging and hitting his shoulder. I go to hit the bald guy again, but another guy blindsides me by putting a bloody hand on the bat. He rips it out of my hand with one snatch.

He's big. At first glance he looks like a thick guy. But he jabs the bat in my side, and I realize he's muscular. He looks young, in his late 20s maybe.

He's got a big face, messy blond hair slicked back, wearing a big black coat over a military green colored sweatshirt and blue jeans. I fall to the ground holding my side, nearly kneeling on his black sneakers. I feel a sting lingering in the jabbed spot. I curl, bracing for a hard blow to my head or neck. But he doesn't hit me again, instead he throws the bat toward the closet.

He then pulls me by my coils with his other hand and tosses me forward near the glass on the floor. It looks like he broke our glass bowl. *Please just let us go. Please, just let us go.*

I hear Olivia pleading to the other guy. I don't know what to do. "Wh-What do you want?" My hands press to the floor, and I look up and he approaches me with a bag. He pulls it over my face, and I try to trip him and rip the bag off me. "Stop! Stop! Get this off. Get this off!" It means nothing to him. He holds me down, a knee on my back, but he's pressing my head down, he's not choking me. The bag is choking me. I hear Olivia scream before everything goes dark.

Chapter 5: Harvey
1985 - WINTER

Two weeks later, I am in Tim and my bedroom wondering how to describe my day. I always write about events like a story. Even though it happens to me, I have this skill where I can write it like it is a character. Like last week:

Instead of it being his dad in the living room in the middle of the night, it was his mom. Her hands covered her face, and her cries softly breathed in and out in the living room. She thought she was alone. And he noticed when she realized she wasn't. She uncovered her face, looked around once and then took an already crumbled napkin and used it to wipe snot from her nose, then her eyes. The sound of her sniffles remained in the air.

He wanted to step into the living room and comfort her. To not ask the stupid question of "What is wrong" and not illogically tell her everything is going to be okay. He just wanted to be there for her. Silently. But he couldn't bring himself to step in the living room. He wondered how long she had been in there crying. Was this the first night or if she had done this before? He only heard her cries from his parents' bedroom. He never saw her in the living room alone, in the middle of the night, with her thoughts.

Today, though, I thought I had nothing to write about, until the lunch lady hit on me. I'm a lanky Black kid who's only slightly above average height. I don't look built like a college student. She had complimented my hair, then asked me how school was going. She had suggested, "You should get the pudding. Or you could just be my pudding, and I'd be just the right spoon to scoop you in. You like to lick the spoon don't you?"

I didn't respond and I didn't grab the pudding.

She said if I ever needed help with studying, I could come to her. She had did a wink. Some kid in my class had overheard and was snickering, but I wanted to get out of there. I had kept saying "Uh-huh. Ok. Uh-huh. Ok," reminding myself to never go up to get lunch on Tuesdays and Thursdays when she was on schedule.

"What are you always writing?" I hear behind me.

I turn around in my chair to see my dad at the door. His stance is wobbly. His eyes are drooped. I know he isn't drunk because, since the accident, Ma got rid of a lot of his alcohol besides the ones that had a little bit left in the bottle. He just finished his last bottle two nights ago. She had told him it was Grandma's doing, and Grandma didn't mind taking the blame. They didn't argue about it. He didn't really comment about it at all.

He yawns, giving more emphasis he is just waking up from a nap.

"Stories," I reply. He usually calls Tim and me to him and Ma's room or downstairs. He never really comes in our room.

"What are you, the next Langston Hughes?"

"He writes poems. I said stories."

My dad steps into the room with a grunt. "Fine. You the next Ralph Ellison? Charles Dickens? Edgar Allen Poe?" He clutches the doorknob and uses his other hand to point at me. "Uh-huh. Bet you didn't think I could throw out other names. Trying to be slick saying he's a poet." He makes his way to my bed and drops down. "Name a playwrighter."

"Ed Bullins and Lorraine Hansberry are playwrights. *The Electronic N****** and *A Raisin in the Sun*." I swallow, unsure what he is going to say about me writing. He knows I pass the time after school getting lost in my notebook.

"I ask for one and you give me two." He
shakes his head and looks back at the door. "A
know-it-all." Returning his stare to me, he asks,
"What are you even writing about?

"My life."

"That's not writing. That's taking notes.
Usually someone's writing about you. They call it a
biography."

I shake my head. "There are also memoirs or
autobiographies. Maya Angelou did it."

"You gonna be the next Maya Angelou?"
He grunts.

"I'm just gonna be Harvey Patts," I answer.
I don't care if he doesn't get it. He doesn't know
what I'm capable of. I can make a name for myself. I
can be a famous writer, a famous author. I could
even teach other guys to get into writing.

There's so much power in storytelling. It's
not just an escape; it's a release and a time capsule of
the world. It's history and shows people we were a
part of it. From Malcolm X, Toni Morrison, to
W.E.B. Du Bois, James Baldwin, Zora Neale
Hurston, and Nella Larsen. There's a reason we read
almost all of them in school. Stories and
perspectives are shown. It's exciting to think my life

could be read and discussed in a classroom and represent the time or family structure, events that took place, or locations that expanded or no longer exist.

My dad stands up and looks at the wall of pictures of Tim and I, and us with friends and family. "There you go again, being smart." He emphasizes the word *smart*, like I'm being slick or sly. Speaking out of turn. But the way he stands, staring at the pictures but not moving his head to glance at other photos—not turning to me to add more to his statement—it feels like a compliment. He hasn't complimented me in years. I dare not question in what way he meant the word *smart*. Instead, I sit and watch him, hoping he might embrace my writing and my goals.

He walks out, pausing to tap the frame of the door with his knuckle. "Be careful with your goals."

I feel the heat rush to my chest. He doesn't support me. "I got this," I manage to say. "My teachers are helping me plan for college and everything."

He turns around. "Teachers. They have their own agendas sometimes."

I don't know what he means. "What agenda do you have?"

He blinks at me. He looks down and then balls his fist. "Don't disrespect me."

"I-I'm not."

He steps back into the room. "You got something you want to say to me? Say it, Harvey."

The anger spreads throughout my whole body. I stand up. He wants me to share what I think? Fine. Yeah, I'll do it. "You make this family feel bad about themselves. You don't want to read my writing or encourage anything I do. You tell Tim he's too much, either with his energy, or talking, or activities. He's a kid who loves you even when you keep nagging on him. Then with Ma, you-you hurt her. Emotionally, mentally . . ." I shake my head. "Why is it so hard for you to be happy and to make us happy, too?"

He shouts, "You think I don't want to be happy?" He takes a step closer. "You think I don't want my family to be happy?"

I don't say anything. I fear how close he'll get to me. My fingers curl into fist as I stand guard.

"Did you ever think about if your mom hurts me? That she hurts me, too?"

A scoff escapes me. "How?" What did she do? What could she have done to him? I shake my head, confused. Why are they together if they hurt each other?

He stares me up and down. He shakes his head, then looks at Tim's side of the room. His shoulder rolls back as his head raises and looks to the ceiling. He lets out an *ah* laugh. "Someone will always be better than you."

I don't know what he's getting at.

"It's hard to live up to other people's expectations, let alone your goals for yourself, Harvey." I watch his right hand. He uses his thumb to press each knuckle per finger, one at a time. He locks eyes with me. "Life." He shakes his head. "Humans make mistakes. It can really screw everything up."

Are we the mistake? Tim and me? Him being with Ma? Is having a family his mistake? But he doesn't say another word to me. He turns around and walks out. I hear the creak of each step as he goes down it.

. . .

Two months later, spring break is just around the corner, and I can get a breather from presentations. I'm about to head to chemistry class when I hear someone bellowing my name. I turn around to see Ma hysterical. She's limping with momentum toward me. She's wearing a green dress with her gray cardigan that has a rip in its shoulder. Her hair is messy; even the clip-on bun is frizzy. My body grows stiff. My heart begins to race. Is it Tim?

"Harvey." She reaches me and lets all her weight fall on me as she cries.

"Ma, what's wrong?" I hold the back of Ma's head and hug her. People look at us as they pass. "What happened, Ma?"

"Your father is dead." She cries. Muffled, I hear, "He was . . . accident."

I hold Ma and watch as students continue to stare. A history teacher I've never had approaches us. The little hand on the clock hanging above the hall moves to each number.

I don't know how his death made me feel. I just know even dead he still left a bad linger on us.

Chapter 6: Lasher
2011 - WINTER

I open my eyes and blink repeatedly. A man is kneeling in front of me, but I can't make out his face just yet. I think it's my dad. My body is leaning on something hard. I strain my eyes wider to get a better look at him.

He taps at my cheek. "Wake up. Come on, wake up kid." It's not my dad. The voice is louder than my dad's, not as timid. And this guy is white.

I start using my arms to push me up off this rough surface, but I'm immediately caught off balance. My arms won't go the way I want them to. It's like they're glued together. I look down and realize I'm handcuffed. My arms are forced out in front of me. My legs extended out as well. To the right of me, is a radiator I'm leaning against.

The man gives me one last slap in the cheek. "There ya go. Look at me." It's the bald guy. He's wearing all black, not a trace of hair on his face besides his thick eyebrows and short eyelashes. He's uncomfortably close to me. "Your Harvey's son, right?"

I swallow. So, this is the guy my dad went to for money? I don't move my head. I don't say anything.

"I'll repeat myself only once. You're Harvey's son, right?" His eyes squint and his lips are pressed together. His arm is extended on the radiator helping him keep his balance.

"Yeah," I mutter.

"Where is he?"

"I don't know."

"Don't do that."

"I don't know," I repeat, clearer. I wish I did. "He was supposed to come back soon."

"He's covering for him," another voice says. I didn't realize behind the bald guy, near a stairway, was the guy that had thrown me to the ground. He looks more average-sized compared to when I first saw him. His hand is bandaged up.

"He didn't tell me where he was going. He didn't even tell me what he did. He just . . . he left."

The bald guy grabs my shirt and looks me in my eyes. "If you don't start talking, I'll have to ask your sister."

My eyes widen. Olivia. "My friend. Where is she? She wouldn't know anything. She was just visiting me. Leave her out of this."

The bald guy moves from my personal space for the first time, revealing Olivia maybe six feet away, handcuffed to a radiator, too.

Why did I let her come over? I should've just waited for my dad alone.

"Please, just let her go," I say. "She's got nothing to do with this."

The bald guy grabs a foldout chair leaning against the cement wall and drags it over to me. He sits, his feet nearly stepping on me.

"We'll see," the long-haired guy says. He turns to Olivia, and she's moving. They don't have her facing me; instead, her back is to the radiator and her arms are handcuffed to the side. She looks from the stairs across from her to our direction.

"She's awake," Long-haired Guy announces.

"Let's see what she knows," the bald guy says.

Olivia's voice is dry. She mutters, "Nothing."

The bald guy grabs my hair, tilting my head toward him. He announces, "He won't tell us where Patts is."

All she knows is that we ran into money problems effecting my tuition and making us lose our house. Why am I even going to a Catholic school? Dad doesn't talk about religion at all, but he makes it seem so important that I go to one and learn faith and be a respectable person. *He should've gone to a Catholic school!* No, I can't get upset right now. Olivia is being questioned about something she knows nothing about.

I had told her my dad was getting a job and I'd hopefully be back soon. But, I had doubted I'd be back. I doubted I'd be able to stay in Pennsylvania. I broke and couldn't keep a hopeful façade. I was scared my dad was going back to his old ways. He hadn't shown signs six months ago, like he has been recently. I didn't want to be right.

"No, no, no, no, no, no, no," is all Olivia can keep muttering.

"So, you know something," Long-haired Guy says. He gets closer to her.

"Stop," I beg.

Her voice sounds clearer when she says, "We don't know anything. I want nothing to do with that man. He has nothing to do with me." She looks at me, staring at how the bald guy won't let me go.

"What did he even do?" I ask.

The bald guy yanks my head forward, until I am looking down at my lap. He screeches the chair even closer, until it's touching me, and I'm uncomfortable between his legs and crotch. I look at him. He bends down in my face. I can smell the coffee and gum on his breath, and it makes me want to vomit. "Your father took my money. Took $10,000 and bet with it, saying we'd make triple."

"Gambling?" Olivia blurts out. She shakes her head while looking at me.

"What do you know?" Bald Guy questions over his shoulder to Olivia. But he's still close to my face, nearly brushing our cheeks together.

"Nothing. I just . . . you're wasting your time. Get him! Not us. We can't fucking help you," she says.

"She wouldn't know anything. She's telling the truth," I say.

"Then, *you* would," Long-haired Guy yells.

I gotta tell them everything I know. This back and forth isn't to mess with him; it's two kids caught in the middle of something that we have no control over. Why can't they see that?

"I knew he started gambling," I say. "I mean technically he off-and-on gambles. But last year it started to feel different. Work cut him and he turned to it. But he lost it all, and we had to move. He couldn't afford me going to school. But instead of finding a new job, he said he'd figure out a way to get it back. He said . . . to trust him. But, I thought he was putting in effort toward the wrong thing. When I tried to call him out, he got mad." I shake my head. "He's in a bad place. It's bigger than you."

"Bullshit," Bald Guy says, pulling back from my face some, but the spit still hits me from how he emphasizes *it*. "He used my sister to get to me. Slept with her and acted like they had something going on, and it was a lie. He did it to make a deal with me, then split. Another lie." Bald Guy is getting red now. The longer he stays in my face, the more I want to pass out. I rest my head on the radiator as an attempt to distance myself from him. "He knew what he was doing."

I shake my head. "I'm sorry. He'll give you your money." I half-believe it; that's why I say it.

"How do you know?"

"I don't. But the last text I got from him was last night. He said he had to take care of some business and may not be back until tomorrow night. Which is tonight. He wasn't running or messing with your money. He probably was working it all out."

"Don't be dumb, boy," Long-haired Guy shouts.

Bald Guy grabs my chin. "He messed with the wrong family." He then whispers in my ear, "I can play his game." I think he's going to punch me in my face, but instead punches me in my ribs. He releases my face, and I curl toward the radiator.

Olivia screams, "No!"

"For the record, you look fucking like him," Bald Guy says, before kicking me in my side.

What did you do Dad? Why did you do it? How are you going to get us out of this? You said you'd be back today. Please, have their money. Please come and help us.

I hear the chair skid back as he gets up, and then stomping up the stairs before the door slams.

"Lash," Olivia calls.

"Yeah," I strain.

"Are you okay?"

I look at her, and I try to smile. To be hopeful. But I feel sickened and worried if I'm bruised or if he cracked anything. I want to try to calm Olivia, but I don't know how to calm myself.

I'm startled when I hear Olivia start screaming, "Help! Help!" She keeps repeating it. She's facing me, trying to stand but the handcuffs limit her.

The basement door flies open. Bald Guy is rushing down the steps with Long-Haired Guy following. I try to sit up more. Olivia is frozen in place.

Bald Guy grabs Olivia's face. "Dumb girl," he snarls. Olivia falls onto her knees. He surprises me when he slaps her. He got her in her cheek and mouth it seems. A sound escapes her in shock. They go back upstairs and lock the door.

Olivia's looking down. I can tell she's crying. I did this to her. I got her in this mess. They're willing to hurt both of us. They don't care if we truly don't have answers about my dad.

"Liv."

She just shakes her head. I don't know what to say.

"I don't want to die," she cries. She sits, curling inward toward herself.

I shake my head now. "We're not."

"They can't do this," she says.

She's right. They shouldn't be able to do this. I close my eyes, trying to wish us out of here. Or at least her.

"My dad's gonna find out I'm missing," she continues.

My eyes pop open. "How? He doesn't even know we still hangout."

"He's going to figure it out."

"*Psssh*." That's farfetched. As much as it would be nice, I can't see it. Olivia barely shares information with her dad, and her dad seems too engrossed in himself to know anything about what she does when she feels lonely.

"It's not like your dad's here to help," she argues.

But there's still a chance. "He will." He wouldn't just leave me.

"Look at the shit we're in, Lasher! Your dad's leaving you to die for him."

"You don't know that. Your relationship with your dad isn't so ideal. It's like he wishes your mom was around and you weren't."

"You're a fucking punching bag! Do you hear yourself? You must be so concussed, Lash. How do you not see this is messed up?" She shakes the handcuffs. "This is messed up."

What does she know? Is it really messed up to try for your son? And if he's doing all this to try to have me have a better future, then it's also my fault. "He cares," I say. I feel tears building in my eyes. I wince as my side stings. "All of this is because he wants to do right for us. He wants a good life for us."

"He abuses you."

"He's family. My mom left us, but he wants me in his life."

"Well, I sure don't like your dad's version of a good life."

She's mocking his choices. She's flat out calling him a bad dad. There's good in him. There has to be. Why am I the only one that sees it?

Do I even believe he's a good dad? I want to. I care about him. I've had enough, though. I'm so tired of worrying. Of fearing.

I hear the noise before I realize it's coming from my mouth. I'm screaming. I kick the chair out my way. I try to pull these handcuffs and break them. I know this isn't good. I know my dad messed up. I start ramming my shoulder into the radiator repeatedly. It feels good because it's like I'm beating away having to feel my feelings about my dad. I just want to feel this pain rather than think negative of him. "THIS IS MESSED UP!"

This time Long-haired Guy comes down, alone. I freeze when I see he's holding a gun. "Shut up," he says. He's stopped on the steps. "I shouldn't hear a peep out of you. I want my money. Not two kids. I don't have to keep you alive for Harvey to see you. I'll do it. It'll be a lesson." He points the gun back and forth between Olivia and me, as he comes off the steps. He then leaves it pointed at me and starts getting closer. He presses the gun on my temple.

Heat rushes to my face, sweat forms on my forehead. My chest is rising and falling. He won't do it. This isn't about us. This is just a threat. I have to believe it's just a threat.

I'm staring at Olivia. Her eyes are wide and tears fall. She dares not speak either. He finally lowers the gun and turns. He stomps back up the steps and then slams the door.

I look down, a tear escapes my eye. I will not die. I will not die. I will not die.

Dad help. Please, help us.

Chapter 7: Harvey
1985 - SPRING

I'm sitting on my bed with my dad's note in my hand. Leaving me something makes that car accident feel less of an accident.

I know you already don't want to be like me. But I'm saying this anyway: don't drink.

I know you're smoking weed with your buddies. Do it for unwinding, sleeping, relaxing. But the second it makes you lose sight of the present. When it makes you want to escape and you can't plan your day or week without it, you've gone too far.

You've got a future. Fight for it better than I did.

I swallow. He gives me the addiction talk as his final words?

I crumble it up but pause. I'm not throwing it away. I unravel it, fold it, and shove it in my wallet, in the back, empty slot. It's the first thing he's given me since I was eleven. "You've got a future" stands out the most. Does he . . . did he really believe that all along? Young me would cherish this. Young me never wanted to throw something from him away. Even if it was a shirt that wasn't my style, but he gave it to me because it couldn't fit him anymore. But now? Now I'm just mad at him.

But why do I care about young me right now? He couldn't even trust us enough to leave us with his mashed potatoes and gravy recipe. He didn't want to make any traditions with his sons. He didn't want to leave something good of his legacy. I was pissed staring at his casket, but I held it in for Tim.

Tim balled at the funeral. He was so sad, and all I could feel was a heavy weight. The whole time I couldn't help but think of the what ifs and the times I wanted my parents to split. They always seemed sad and worried together.

Tim comes into the room. He has what looks like a mac and cheese stain on his pajama shirt. For two days straight, he's been eating the leftover food from the funeral as a coping mechanism. Mom barely eats. To my surprise, he has a small smile on his face. He hands me a notepad size, lined paper, with the top edge still frazzled from being ripped out.

"What's this?" I ask.

"The mashed potatoes recipe," he says. He sits across from me on his bed. It squeaks a little as he plops down.

I hand it back to him, shaking my head, not glancing at it. I lean back and partially chuckle. I look away from Tim and let my finger rest between my lips. He actually shared the recipe. I lick my bottom lip and look at Tim. "He gave it to you? Unbelievable."

"You never really cooked in the kitchen. You cleaned, killed the bugs for us, stocked the cabinets and fridge. But you're no cook."

"I know how to cook some things."

"I help mom cook more than you do."

I nod. It's true; I just wish I got something more sacred than a letter. I hold out my hand, now ready to see the recipe.

It really is *the* mashed potato recipe. The ingredients. His handwriting. All he said to Tim was:

I know I wasn't the best, but at least this is. When you grow up, your family will have you and your cooking. Don't make my mistakes.

I look at Tim. "And you're satisfied with this?"

Tim shrugs. "It's the recipe, HP."

I nod. "Yeah. Here I was thinking the whole time he didn't want to leave us anything good. You got the good end of the stick."

Tim shakes his head. "Don't say that. He's dead."

I hand it back to him.

He takes it and puts it under his pillow. Like it's a tooth or something.

"You remember busting your lip and losing a tooth?" I ask.

"Only a little."

"You got stitches and everything."

"I feel it sometimes. It's rare, but it reminds me it happened."

"Yeah. Can't even see it now."

He smiles wide. "Uh-hmm. That's 'cause my smile is still great and another tooth grew in."

I shake my head. "I never once had to go to the hospital. Not once."

"Lucky you. You're immune to injury."

We fall into a silence. Should I tell him about the letter Dad left me? It's not as significant as the recipe though. It's him trying to give advice and be a parent. He's late.

Tim says, "Did you know Dad got stitches too? I don't remember my fall, I just remember being at the hospital, bleeding, and feeling so scared. I thought the stitches would be more painful than the fall. To calm me, Dad told me his story. He was eleven. It was on his ear."

I let my tongue roll across my upper teeth. "Dad told you that?"

"Yeah."

I sit up more. "You got all the stories . . . with him. Maybe that's why you liked him more than I did. He shared things with you."

He shrugs and looks down at his feet. "But I don't remember him ever saying he loved us." He looks at me. "Did he ever say it?"

I look up at the ceiling to try to remember. Yeah. Wow, I forgot about that. I look at Tim and can't help but smile. "He did use to say it. When we were going to bed . . ." I chuckle. "I can't even lie and say it was because of you, because you were always dozing off. But Ma used to have him come in to make sure we were going to bed. Before he would leave out the door, I would make him turn back and say, 'I love you.' He said it every time."

But when did that stop? It feels like that was so long ago. Was I eight? Nine?

"That sounds like a good memory," Tim says.

I nod. "It actually is."

Chapter 8: Lasher
2011 - WINTER

My stomach growls, and I look down at it. My body's mad at me. I haven't been treating it right. "I've been so nervous all day I haven't eaten," I tell Olivia. But it's not just today that I haven't eaten. "I told myself I'd eat when my dad got home tonight. That things would be alright once he was home." *Tsk.* "Now look at us."

"Lash . . ." Olivia starts, but her voice trails off.

"He told me if I ever worried about him or us, to tell him. So, I did, and he got mad. So, I can't tell him. Instead, I need to just trust him. And when I can't do that, I get inside my head, and I test how far my trust can go. Sometimes not sleeping until things are better. Sometimes slapping myself every time I doubt him. And sometimes not eating until things are okay."

I hear her swallow. "I'm sorry," she says.

"Saying it out loud . . . I hear how messed up it is." It's the truth.

I look in her direction, but I can't see her. It's nighttime now, and the only light was coming from two windows.

"It's just not fair," I say.

"What isn't?" she asks.

"If I believe that my dad doesn't care about me, then I live in a world where nobody cares about me."

"That's not true. I do."

"The school doesn't. Shouldn't they have followed up with why I didn't come back? Shouldn't his anger management therapist have stayed in touch with him even when we moved? When the neighbors hear yelling and arguing that lasts thirty minutes straight, aren't they supposed to do something because they can't take the noise and maybe, whoever's inside that apartment can't take it either?" I pause, trying to ignore the pain in my side. "I don't matter unless I'm with him. No matter what he does to me, I matter to him. And that's more than anybody shows me."

"I thought things were going to be fine, Lasher. I believed you when you said he was looking for a job. I believed you when you said his anger wasn't out of control. I . . . I didn't know. You can't blame me for not knowing—"

I hear her, but I don't. I want to finish, so I cut her off. "Ya know, I was happy to move back here. I believed my dad was, too. But when he got fired it messed him up. I told him we should just go back to Virginia. He said he didn't want to look like a failure. Actually, he didn't say it flat out, I just knew it was what he meant. He wanted to handle it on his own. He doesn't have many friends." I sigh. "He's so bad with his words." I look at the handcuffs, kind of seeing them in the dark. I can't picture myself getting so upset I almost hit someone and definitely not actually hit anyone. Even if I was being attacked, I can't see myself winning a fight. "His anger destroys the house."

Olivia's voice is low as she says, "The first time I came over when school started, I would have done something if I knew. I would've called my dad or 911." I hear her sniff. She's crying. "You matter to me. Please. You're my friend, Lash. One of my best friends."

I don't know how to respond to that. What type of friend am I? I got Olivia into this mess. I should've known anything could happen when my dad and gambling mixed together. But I selfishly wanted company at a time like this. I let this get out of hand.

It was going downhill before the summer. I knew him telling the principal to give him until July was a sign that I wasn't going back to school. I knew before that, in May, when my dad insisted we walk to Wesley's Diner and eat out. He had smelled like weed. He had been fun and lively, but I could tell something was off. He had been escaping something. I didn't know what. The walk there, he had been cracking jokes, telling me stories, sharing how we should bond more. But the walk back home, it was rainy and silent.

When I asked him if he wanted to watch a show together, he'd said no. At the house, when I had asked if he still wanted ice cream, he'd said no. I had still got a bowl, but I'd eaten it in my room. He'd rolled another blunt and smoked it near the window. I had closed the door because I was scared to know what his demeanor meant. I hadn't wanted to. I watched *Shameless* and left the bowl in my room. I dared not go to the bathroom until three in the morning when I had woken up. He had been curled on the pullout couch, the sheets barely covering his bare feet. But I had told myself he must've had a bad day and kept falsely believing things were still okay.

I don't know how long I've been stuck in my head. I wonder if Olivia is still awake. "Olivia?" no response. "Liv?"

She must've dozed off. I cross my legs and rest my head on the freezing radiator. I try to make out anything in the black void, but the moon isn't even shining on this side to illuminate down here.

I breathe in and out. In and out trying to stop shivering. I also gotta pee. But I shake my head, trying not to think about all these things. *No, forget about my body. Where's my dad? Did you make it home, Dad? Did they call you?* That's when I remember I had my cellphone in my pocket. I elbow my pockets now, but it's not there. Did they take it? Did they call him and tell him they have us? He knows I'd never call. I'd never burden him unless it was dire. They probably called. That's good and bad. It's good because my dad will know what he has to do. He'll give them the money. But it's bad because if my dad comes here, they could do anything. They may actually kill us. Or kill him.

I gulp down saliva I wish was big enough to warm my whole body. But thinking of my dad being killed just makes me colder. It just makes me want to figure out a way to escape, so I can tell my dad to run. To not listen to them or come. To not give them the money.

I can't make noise because those guys will come, and they might actually just kill us. I don't know what they have planned. Who am I anyway? A dropout? A son of a thief? My life's going nowhere. But what about Olivia? I'm a bad friend, too. I let my fingers chip at the radiator. I can't hit myself in these handcuffs. I can't smack myself out of this. I close my eyes. Pressing my eyelids tightly shut.

I can't! I hear screams in my head. A woman's voice. My mom's. She rushes out the door, leaving it open. Her straight-and-press being blown back when she throws the door open. She zipped up her favorite, ugly, powder blue fleece before rushing out of sight. Her scent lingered for an hour. Artificial strawberries. It smelt like one of those dolls she collected with food for a name.

That night, my dad and I burned them because I couldn't sleep, and I told him it was because of their big heads creeping me out. Really, it was because of their awful smell. We went to sleep smelling like firewood instead.

I go to lay down, but I'm in the apartment. I'm not a kid anymore. I'm in bed under the covers, looking at the door. It's closed, but I want my dad to come in. I want to know he's okay. I start to doze off and jolt myself awake. I have to see him come through the door. I blink. I think about turning, but my body is stuck on my side, one arm out the covers, my other arm underneath the pillow. The coolness underneath the pillow usually would refresh me, but this time it's too cold. It feels like a freezer. I want to put the blanket over my arms, but I see the handle jiggle. It's slow, but it's turning. It keeps turning. Instead of the door opening my eyes do.

I blink awake into bluish darkness. I'm confused until I lift my head and feel a dent of the radiator pressing into the side of my face. I had fallen asleep and used it like a hard pillow. I look at the small rectangle windows above us. Daylight is slowly coming. It must be like 4 a.m. Maybe 5 a.m. I look around the basement and the sky helps me just make out Olivia's silhouette.

I gotta think of a plan. I shouldn't be sleeping. How could we get outta here? How do people get out handcuffs in movies? Butter and slide out the handcuffs? No. They pick the handcuffs with like a toothpick or bobby pin. Yes. That's it. Olivia might have one of those. But how would she get it out of her hair? But, what if she has it in her pockets? What if she doesn't have one at all? I stare at my gray and white shoes, my one undone shoelace. Could that work?

"Lash?" Olivia's voice is snakelike and rapid.

I blink out of my thoughts. Confused if I really had heard it.

"Lash?" This time Olivia's voice is trembling.

She's cold. It's wintertime, and we're stuck in a freezing basement. I sigh. "I'm sorry, Liv. I'm sorry you're here."

I hear her moving her legs. "Lash . . . if I weren't here, you'd be here alone. Then it would be even harder to find you."

I move my legs to a crisscross position. This is my family's mess. "You still shouldn't be here," I say.

"I am. We're past that. I just had a dream about my dad."

"Yeah?"

"He listened to me. He hugged me, and I could feel a difference in him. I couldn't talk though. He said he loved me, and I couldn't respond."

I couldn't do anything in my dream, either. Couldn't say anything to my mom. Couldn't even stay long enough to see my dad come through the door.

"Do you hate your dad, Lash?"

I suck in a breath and let it out slowly. The truth. I need to practice the truth. "De–Depends on the day. I blame him for mom leaving. But I blame her too. I was a kid and she cared about her safety and not mine. I blame my dad when I feel lonely or sad or confused. But then I know he wants things for me. He wants me to achieve things and be . . ." Be something he never got to see or achieve with his family. "Last year he told me he didn't finish high school. That I'd be the first male Patts to do so. My dad's dad didn't finish, and he doubts his grandpa did. My dad's brother didn't finish, either. I asked him why, but he never told me. But what I understood is that what I do matters to him. He wants something for me that he didn't have."

I lick my lips. "I've always felt like he wanted me to leave him, but that he loved and hated me for staying." I shake my head. "I'm not surprised he turned to any means to try to get me back in school. I just wish it were another way."

"I don't think I'll ever understand," she admits.

"I know." My stomach growls.

She sighs. "What time do you think it is?"

"Late. Early, depending on how you look at it," I reply.

"I gotta pee."

"Sleep can help you forget about it."

"I don't want to go back to sleep. I don't trust here. I didn't mean to fall asleep before."

"I had dozed off, but I had a dream about my mom. She was yelling, so I woke up," I say.

"I barely remember my mom. I can picture her clearly. Her face, her hair, how she dressed, but I don't really remember her. I don't remember what she was like. The stories my dad and aunt used to share . . . It always felt like they were talking about someone I wish I met." She pauses. "You can dream of your mom yelling, and I can't even remember my mom's voice. Well, that's not true. I remember her laugh." She laughs. "She had this loud laugh. So loud."

I chuckle. I can hear Olivia smiling as she remembers her mom. I'm glad she has a happy memory.

"But words? No. I can still feel her hug, though, when I think about it closely. One hand on my back. The other hand on the back of my head. Squeeze. Kiss on top of my head."

"Sounds like she was loving."

She doesn't say anything after that. I don't want her mom's love to leave the space, so I don't say anything either. Instead, I try to feel that hug she just described. Feel less alone. Feel loved.

. . .

But I can't doze off again. I can't get warm or comfortable. I can't shake the fact my dad is spiraling again. Can he not do anger management checkups every year or month? When I was a kid, and he was in the anger management group, they had these community events at the place. The guys were always encouraged to go. I always thought of it as a family meet and greet. Mingling and seeing other kids that understood my situation. It was weird, because all our dads were getting happier there through help. Our dads were becoming this other person, that we thought fought away the bad versions of themselves. And we believed it truly only worked because they had each other. I believed it was the power of a forced friendship. When the program was over, they planned a gathering. We ate and played games. I never saw my dad so . . . open. It was like he was happy with life. That made me hopeful for our future. That life would be fine without my mom.

But something changed when he overheard me speaking to Declan. He had asked if I saw my cousins or visited my grandparents. I told him I didn't see any of my family members. It was just my dad and me. Us together. I turned to my dad and smiled, but he looked at me with a serious face. His mustache full, hair picked out, and eyes glaring straight into mine. Searching for something I didn't have to give. He hadn't looked that serious in months. He put down his cup and walked away to the bathroom.

I looked back at Declan, and he said, "Maybe you'll see your extended family this year."

I knew I wouldn't, but I played along and said, "Yeah."

By the time I turned thirteen, we moved from Virginia back to Pennsylvania. Just the two of us. Dad was still cheery. He said he wanted me to be able to go back to the place I had started growing up in. But in the back of my mind always lingered questions I never asked. Why couldn't I live where my dad grew up? Why couldn't I see his home? Why did he never take me to Massachusetts? Does his family even know I exist?

It always made me wonder if I was enough for him. I try hard to be enough and show him I love him, but he looks at me in those moments as if I were told to say, "I love him", or stick around. Like I gave him a prize for coming in last. I don't try to look at him with pity, just curiosity and questions I know not to ask. I always wonder what he truly thinks of me, and if I make him happy at all.

I must've fallen asleep with my eyes open or was thinking too hard because I snap back into reality when I hear my name whispered in the air. I blink, and that's when I realize it's daylight in the basement. I can see Olivia, and she has tears running down her face. She sniffs, and I blink again. I curl my legs close to me, feeling the brisk air rush into my body.

"It's cold." My jeans feel like they are frozen to me.

She nods with a sniff. "I know." She looks at the stairs. Is she crying because it's cold or something else? I can't manage to ask her. My fists are tightly squeezed.

"I don't hear them," she says.

I manage to unfreeze enough to shrug. "Could mean . . . anything."

Her stomach growls now. She starts to shake, and she curls into herself, searching for warmth. She uses her shoulder to wipe her tears. We fall into a cold silence. I wish we were near each other. We could hug for warmth. She stares at me and lets out a breath. Her shadow on the ground looks small. Can't tell her head from hair. It all just blends as one. Thinking of her hair, I remember the bobby pin. A possible way to escape.

"Do you have a bobby pin?" I ask.

She looks to the side thinking, then sighs. "No."

"Do you see anything like a paperclip on the floor or something as flexible?"

We both look around. I will myself to adjust from the stiff position. I try not to invite the cold in more by moving. I stretch my feet every which way to see if I feel anything. I then get on my knees and try to peer under the radiator.

"I'm not seeing anything," she says.

"Ugh, neither am I."

"We can't just sit here. Waiting for them to do something." She gets to her feet, bending over because the handcuffs don't allow us to stand upright. "We gotta try something." She yanks at the radiator.

It's worth a shot. I stand, too, hunched over. I pull, yank, strain.

We freeze at the noise of our grunts and look at the door. Surprisingly, no one comes. There's no sound of movement upstairs. I look at Olivia, and she's already staring at me. I shrug. This may be our chance to try everything to escape. "Let's keep going."

We pull. We yank. We bang. We scream. We sit. We push. We strain. We wiggle. I kick. I give up last.

Nothing worked. These old radiators won't break. I don't want to look at her, but she's right across from me. I choose to look down at the floor instead. The dusty, cold, cement floor. Snot dripping off my nose. I sniff it up only for it to slide back down again. My chest rises and falls. It's so quiet. Where did those guys go? Where is my dad? Hell, where is Olivia's dad? Is he looking for her?

I look at the sky, and it's probably afternoon. The sun is far, but at least it's shining. At least it's providing some comfort to this awful situation.

Chapter 9: Harvey
1986 - SPRING

It sucks being in that in-between stage, where I'm seventeen but not a senior yet. I want to graduate already. But, at least I got my friends. We're in the school stairwell hanging out.

"Remember when Carla did the loudest fart during a math test," Lee says.

Carla hits him. "Shut up. That was so embarrassing."

I laugh and stick some chips in my mouth.

"Not as embarrassing as Ed being told in front of the whole class that he scored a seventeen in Chemistry," Will says.

"That was sad," Carla says. She reaches to take some chips from me.

"Come on y'all. You're forgetting the number one embarrassing moment," Owen states. "When Harvey's mom came running, well to the best of her ability, down the hall to tell him his dad died."

"Come on, man. That's not funny," Lee says.

I put the chips down. "You think that's funny?" I look at Owen, sitting a step higher, diagonal from me.

"We're talking about embarrassment. I was saying embarrassing." He slyly smirks.

I shake my head and stand. "You said running to the best of her ability. I heard that comment."

"Oh, give me a break," Owen says.

I slide over to him and grab his shirt. "Don't talk about my ma."

"Then can I talk about your dad?" Owen replies.

I punch Owen in the face. Then do it again. Owen falls against the railing.

"Harvey, stop." Lee grabs my shoulder and arm, pulling me back.

…

At home, Ma doesn't get it.

"Why are you fighting?" Ma asks.

"Owen was being smart. He was talking about you."

"Then tell him off, not punch him out. You got suspended."

I shake my head. "He's an asshole."

"You know better."

I'm silent. I do, but I'm not gonna let anyone talk about my family.

"You're a role model to your brother. Becoming a man faster than you can understand. But, I need you to do the right thing."

I nod once.

"I know your father always told you to be more street smart, but you don't have to get like this because he's not here."

"It's not about him," I tell her. I walk off to my room.

. . .

Three months later, it's the summer, and I finished junior year.

Lee and I are sitting on the porch at his house. Kids ride bikes down his block. The sun is beaming, and the smell of laundry detergent is seeping out of the neighbor's house. Lee's crushing an ice cream sandwich while I'm eating an ice pop.

"You always eat ice cream like it's gonna be taken from you?" I ask.

"It melts! It's hot. I'm eating it before it's just milk and chocolate," he says while chewing.

I shake my head. "Sticky hands. Crumbs all over your face."

"Excuse me for not being Professor Patts over here, sucking the ice pop every three minutes."

I half smile. "Professor? You think I could be a professor?"

He tries to use the outer part of the wrapper to wipe off his hands. "Maybe. If you chilled out a little more, got a nice haircut instead of that lengthy wild thing, and bought better shoes. I could see you looking like an uptight professor at some college."

"I wouldn't be uptight."

"Students would fear you."

I smile proudly. "Then my job is done."

He chuckles. "We're seriously about to be on that path. Graduating and shit. Living on a college campus without our moms. Being taught the stuff we actually want to know. Then we're gonna be looking for jobs? Where did the time go?"

I swallow. "Taking the SAT made it real for me, man. That shit was awful."

"Visiting college was no joke. One campus felt like what you see in the movies. The way it looked nice, students walking by and heading to classes or their dorm buildings. It felt so big, and I felt small."

"You ain't small," I assure him.

"Thanks. Neither are you. I hope you, your mom, and Tim are gonna look at some of your colleges this summer."

I take another inhale of the ice pop. He doesn't know we can't afford all that traveling. I'm probably gonna stay local. Lee didn't choose any local schools. None of our schools really overlapped when I was looking at the states he was thinking about. D.C., Virginia, Florida, New York. He's going for Business and Economics. I'm going for Creative Writing, Screenplays. I tried looking at a school in New York, but that crowded life ain't for me. Local is better, so I can be there for Tim and Ma.

"I'm staying in Massachusetts."

He looks at me. "That's it? You're not considering leaving anymore?"

"I want to be near ma and Tim."

He swallows and sits back. "Yeah." He touches the brick of his house with the back of his hand. "Me being an only child and my mom being a child of five, she encouraged getting out and exploring. I know she'll be alright. But we're in different situations. I get it."

I nod. "At least I got an excuse to get out of this state and visit you."

He holds out his fist with a smile and I bump it.

. . .

He was excited for senior year. For graduating and starting a new chapter of his life. To feel like he got to finally figure out what he can do in this world.

But before his senior year could start, he dropped out of school in August because Ma needed him to work. He thought he was helping by working at a family friend's barbershop, sweeping and cleaning. But the $2.50 an hour pay proved to not be enough when one evening at home the water got cut off. It was the beginning of November, and the temperature was brisk. No water meant no radiators warming up for heat. He told his ma he had to find a real job. That's when he started working at Shoe Shop five days a week.

What he didn't expect was his last paycheck from Shoe Shop near the end of winter. Some people broke into the store and robbed them overnight. They destroyed the place and took 70 percent or 80 percent of the shoes. His boss said the amount of money lost and the repairs needed was a thin line between closing the store or getting it back up and running. The boss decided to let everyone go, and that must've meant he was letting go of the shop, too.

School-less and jobless wasn't an option for him, so he looked for jobs quick. He wound up at Kitchen Wing plus asked around if anyone needed to be tutored. It was nice for him to still be doing something school related.

But the niceness quickly wore off knowing so many kids were in school, and he wasn't one of them. His best friend told him about the colleges he and other people in their grade was getting into. He applied to two and ma told him not to retract them. If they decided on their own to drop him, so be it, but she wanted him to *still be able to go to college. The waiting game to hear back was nerve-wracking. But, not being in school, and the thought of not walking on that dumb black stage, was irritating him more and more.*

Both colleges contacted the school, and the school told them of his leave. One college put him on a waiting list, the other didn't consider him because he didn't get his diploma.

...

At graduation, I watch Lee and Carla cross the stage. I clap, I stand, but I can't cheer. My voice fails because I fear if I cheer it would come out as a yell. My hands would cling to the chair in front of me, my voice would echo, and my mouth would be wide open in animosity. So, I clap. Standing there, staring blankly ahead at their smiles toward the crowd.

Chapter 10: Lasher
2011 - WINTER

I open my eyes, and the sky is fading to dark. I can only see Olivia a little. She looks like she's asleep. Great. We're playing the waiting game. Doing nothing but taking turns listening out and falling asleep. We need to get out of here. If they do find my dad, I don't know what will happen. I don't know if they'll let Olivia go. My stomach hurts. Not because I'm starving, but because my dad may have our deaths on his hands. It's one thing to put himself in danger. But why me? Does he know about Olivia being here too? Does he care?

He wouldn't leave me to die. He wouldn't do that. I repeat it over and over again in my head to remind myself that he loves me. My hand wants to jerk toward my face, but it can't. I use my shoulder to rub my cheek and remind myself he's coming.

…

I'm awakened by a kick at my foot. I look up to see the bald guy. They're back. I hear someone come down the steps, and I blink. I open my eyes wide. Daylight is in the basement again. I'm surprised to see two guys coming down the stairs. If

Bald Guy is here, then who's that? My heart starts to pound.

He's here? I wish I could rub my eyes. I blink again, and it's him. My dad is here. His shirt's got blood on it; he doesn't look like he's slept. His lip is busted, and he's barefoot. They didn't cuff him like they did us. His hair is ragged, and his facial hair is more noticeable. He looks like he fought and . . . I swallow.

He doesn't look at me. I don't know what to say. Long-haired Guy is behind him. Did he give them the money? Did he call the cops? Are we doomed? Did he do it? Did he fix this mess? Is he mad at me? Is he mad? Are we going to get out of here? *Dad, look at me. Tell me.*

As he comes off the last step he looks at Bald Guy instead. "You got the money." He needs to clear his throat. To swallow his saliva. "Release them," he continues.

Long-haired Guy pushes him onto his knees. My dad catches himself with his hands, and he keeps staring at the floor. His thick brows are all I can see. Bald Guy is talking while flailing a gun, but I can't hear him. Long-haired Guy has a gun pointed at my dad. At the back of his head. I'm shaking my head.

Then Olivia speaks. She's screaming. She's screaming at my dad. I want to tell her to stop. To not get my dad killed. That he can handle this. That he's figured out something. But, I still can't speak. Why won't he look at me?

I tune in at Olivia's last words. "Look at you. This is seriously all you're gonna do?"

Dad continues to stare. To listen to her. To acknowledge her.

"Look at him!" she screams.

But instead, he looks down, shaking his head. He's crying, sounding like a soft seal. I recognize it because I always thought it didn't fit who he was. Seal cries are so loud, so needy, so sad. He never wants to be that person. Or at least show it. But, maybe that's why it's the sound of his cry. His cry says what he cannot.

When he looks up, he looks in my direction. The lower parts of his eyes are red. He's got snot dripping from his nose. His mouth droops down even though he tries to fight it. They're gonna kill us anyway. My dad couldn't stop this. He was trying. Trying so hard to be someone he couldn't be.

"I'm sorry, Dad," I cry out, tears forming.

"Uh-uh," Dad grunts, shaking his head. "Uh-uh."

"Give him a reason to cry," Bald Guy says to Long-haired Guy.

"No," Dad yells, spit flying out his mouth. I think Long-haired Guy was going to shoot me, but I don't know because my dad throws his body backwards onto him. Long-haired Guy falls, but a shot goes off. I curl against the radiator in fear. Except I'm not hit. Bald Guy screams out in pain. He got shot somewhere.

While he's caught off guard, I wrap both my legs around him and trip him. He falls forward, the gun skidding out his hand. I try to keep him on the floor, holding him with my legs, but he wiggles and kicks out of my grasp. Then, he kicks me in my hip and then again in my leg. Each time, I bang into the radiator.

When I look up, my dad and Long-haired Guy are rolling over each other, back and forth, punching each other. I look at Olivia and she's trying to get the gun that fell out of Bald Guy's hand. But he crawls to the gun, smearing blood from his wound. He gets his hand on the gun and stands. My dad somehow ends up in seated position against the stairwell, Long-haired Guy has him in a chokehold. Baldy pushes Long-haired Guy off my dad, releasing him, then points the gun at my dad.

"STOP!" I yell.

But at the same time, he spits out something to my dad.

My dad coughs, and his wheezes are loud. His chest is rising and falling. He looks at me, slowly shaking his head. "I love you," he mouths.

Tears spill from my eyes. "I-I love you." I'm panting it; it's not audible. "Dad. Dad," I try saying, but it's too soft. I don't know if I'm thinking it or mouthing it.

My dad hears and sees none of this. He's looking at Olivia. He says something to her. But it happens so abruptly. The bald guy shoots my dad in his chest. He shoots him twice. The first shot my dad's chest is rising and falling faster. But the second shot, it slows him down. His breathing keeps slowing down.

"Noooo," is all I can scream. I can't even hold him. I can't help him. I'm choking on my spit, trying to get closer to him. Trying to break these handcuffs.

His stained T-shirt is soaked in blood. I can't hear anything around me but a ringing.

D-i-i-i-i-i-i-i-i-i-i-i-i-i-i-i-n-g.

His head is down. His right hand lies turned up on the ground. But his left hand, is on his lap. His whole body is still. There's no movement. I just want a trace of him to be alive. A finger twitch. A smidge of a foot movement. His mouth to open. For him to just move his head in my direction. He can't go like this.

I'm startled when a shot breaks my concentration. I look up, and officers are on the steps. Bald Guy stumbles to the back of the basement past me. Bald Guy shoots at the officers. An officer with short blonde hair is down, but I look to the left of me, so is Bald Guy. A officer must have shot at the same time as him. He's not dead though. He's been shot in his shoulder. He's lying on the floor, yelling in pain.

I stare at him. He keeps yelling. He had the money, and he chose to do this. To kill my dad. To still keep us handcuffed. He chose this for himself. He shouldn't be screaming. I should be screaming. I've been waiting for my dad to come home for days. I've been waiting to get back to a normal life. I've been waiting to eat. I've been torturing myself and this fucker is hollering.

"SHUT UP!" I scream at him. There's an officer leaning over him, putting him in handcuffs. "SHUT UP!"

The officer turns to me. He looks like he's from a different decade with his long-legged black pants and blue police shirt. He's an oldish Black man with a grandfatherly tone. "You're okay now, son," he says.

I'm not his son. I stare at him, my mouth open, too puzzled to say anything.

"We're gonna get you guys out those handcuffs," the officer continues. He lifts Bald Guy off the ground and takes him towards the stairs.

I turn to Olivia, and she's curled up. Her eyes are squeezed shut. Her shoulder is pressed to her ear, and she's pressed against the radiator as if holding onto it for dear life. When she opens her eyes again, her body is shaking. Before I can gather up something to say, her legs give out and uncurl. Her body slides down along the radiator, and her head falls forward.

"Hey. Hey! Help her!" I beg. I look near Olivia, past her, at a female officer forcing Long-haired Guy to his feet. She brings him up the steps with handcuffs. There's some blood on the wall, a line slanting up, from the blonde officer that had been shot. He's no longer there.

Another officer comes rushing down; he has a medical bag with him. He assesses the basement and then goes to my dad. He places the bag down. He checks my dad's pulse. He shakes his head as the oldish officer comes back down the steps.

He goes to Olivia and checks her pulse. He raises Olivia's head gently and opens her eyelids and then lets them shut. He pulls out a key and then unhandcuffs her. The oldish officer lifts Olivia's unconscious body off the ground and carries her up the steps.

I don't see Olivia and the officer disappear through the door because the medical officer catches my attention.

"Are you hurt?" He bends down in front of me.

He's a blur of my vision as I look past him to my dad.

"Hey. Can you look at me? Are you hurt?"

I slowly turn my head toward him and have to blink to unblur him. He's white. I feel snot and hot tears falling down my face. I don't know. My head is shaking.

He reaches for the handcuffs, not touching me. He undoes them, and my arms fall. I still feel the metal against my wrist. I look down at my hands, seeing if I really have control over them again. "I'm going to help you up now." He doesn't wait for me to respond. He grabs my arm and brings me to my feet. "We're gonna get you checked out."

I shake my head. He walks, pulling me with him, but I push his hand off and fall to my knees in front of my dad's still body.

"I'm sorry. He's gone," the officer says, standing at my side.

What happened? I try to ask my dad with my mind.

I can't leave him. He'll be alone. He can't leave me. What am I supposed to do? He left *me* alone. He left me with no one. He didn't have a plan. He never had a plan.

Chapter 11: Harvey
1987 - SUMMER

"Come on, Harvey. I'm not playing. Take your brother to your Uncle Roger's, then go over to Mr. Hudson's home and see what work he needs done. Make some cash."

"I'm not helping that old man. Come on, Ma."

"I don't see you taking work seriously. Got fired from Kitchen Wing because you were talking back to customers. Got a good job tutoring, but you're too busy flirting."

"The boy snitched. He was a brat."

Ma shakes her head. "Always blaming someone else."

"It's true."

"You need to keep a job."

"People need to get a better attitude so someone will want to serve them."

"Look at you . . . that sounds like something—" she stops herself. She looks away.

My heart starts to pound and heat immediately rises in my fist, up my arms, skipping my neck and going straight to my face. I know what she was going to say. "Don't ever say I'm like him."

She looks at me again. "Then don't become him." She grabs my face. "Harvey, don't become him."

I have wondered what my dad would say about me and the situation we're in. Call me weak? Laugh that I'm trying to be the man of the house? Laugh and say I'm trying to be like him. He didn't graduate high school, and I never thought that would be me.

"I'm gonna help, Ma. I didn't drop out because I couldn't handle school. I didn't like that you quit because of your limp and not being able to move around like you used to. You're struggling, too, looking for a job. I wanted to help." I shake my head. "I wanted you to be able to afford your medication so you wouldn't be in so much pain. I wanted one less financial thing for you to worry about and school made sense to drop."

"I know. I know." She hugs me. "Doesn't mean I like it." She sighs. "Summers almost over. We have to find jobs."

I nod. "We will."

"Did you hear back from that contest?"

I've been applying to writing contests to keep me in my writing mood. My English teacher introduced me to one my sophomore year for teens. I wasn't a part of the top three winners, but I was one of the top three honorable mentions. They gave all six of us feedback. This year I applied to three contests. One I mailed in a creative writing piece I did last year. The other two I mailed in a piece from my book I've been writing about my life. I chose to submit the funeral piece.

"I came in as runner-up," I tell her.

She holds my shoulders. "There you go. Did you win something?"

I sigh. "No. Just a free copy of the magazine."

She sighs and let's go of me. "I'm glad you're still applying. One will hopefully choose you and pay you."

I nod. "I'm getting close."

Two days later, I hear back from the chain, Appetizers. They hired me as their delivery guy. We all are ecstatic that we barbecue in the backyard to celebrate. We didn't use the grill all summer, so it's nice to have a good reason to not let it go to waste.

Dad never used it. It was always me and Ma on the grill. The only time I helped with cooking.

When Ma goes in the house to grab condiments, Tim says, "Come on. You don't gotta do summer reading or nothing. It's not fair. Just let me drop out like you."

"No. No way. Ma needs you to graduate. Shit, I need you to graduate. Us Patts need to make a name for ourselves. You're gonna do it. Got it?"

Tim nods. "Alright, alright. But every good report card I want . . ."

"An endless supply of cheese curls and $20. I know."

Tim smiles. "And if you last long at this job, I hope the free food will come in clutch."

"You and Ma both."

"Hey, since I'm doing this school thing for you. Can you do something for me?"

I turn to him. "What, wise guy?"

"Keep this one. You're just delivering food. Stay focused, HP."

I nod. "Okay. I hear you." I tap his arm with my fist. "I got you."

Tim nods. "Ain't no shame in being a thirty-year-old who goes back to get his high school diploma, anyway."

"Wow. Pushing me all the way to thirty. You think you're funny."

Tim laughs and nudges me with his shoulder. His wide smile, never afraid to show his teeth.

But it sucks to know I am disappointing him in some way with all these job hops. I don't want my brother having to step me aside and tell me to keep a job. I'm supposed to be the example.

How do I be better?

Chapter 12: Lasher
2011 - WINTER

I'm in a hospital bed. I lie on my side and look out the window. My nurse said Olivia woke up. That her dad's with her. But no one's with me. Child Protective Services is coming. I don't want to see them. I just want to lay here. Lay here for a while.

They had to sedate me to get me out of the basement. I didn't want to leave. I couldn't. Because then it would be real. How is this real?

It's Christmas. A holiday meant for gifts, family time, and happy spirits. Yet, I'm getting something worse than coal. Just screw the Patts and their happiness, right? We don't deserve peace? We don't need presents, smiles, and warmth?

The nurse brought me dinner last night and breakfast this morning, but I don't have an appetite. It's like I'm entering this world for the first time, with the knowledge of what should be, but I have a different reality. It's all unfamiliar. How do I even exist? They say a detective is going to come by. For what? They're too late. They should've done their job the day Olivia and I were taken. They should've got all their answers then. Then, maybe the outcome

would've been different. Or made more sense.
There's nothing to say anymore. There's nothing
more they can do.

It's not like they're going to kill the bald
guy for me. There's no revenge, just questions. Just
dumb questions. At the end of the day, they can't
help me. I'll still end up in the foster system. No
mom. No dad. No family. What's the point? I sit up
and search the room. Is there a way I can just end it?

I look at the window again. I'll drop. I'll be
weightless and feel and hear nothing but air. I'll start
falling faster and then I'll hit. I'll be gone, too. No
one has to try to all of a sudden to give a damn about
me. I'm an anonymous boy who will remain
anonymous.

I get off the bed. I walk up to the window
and place my hand on it. It's cold. It sends a chill up
my arm to the back of my neck and down my back. I
remember the basement. I remember it's winter.
This hospital is warm. I place my other hand on the
window. This hospital wants me to forget, but the
window reminds me of his cold body in the
basement. It was still. It was lifeless. Why am I so
mad? He wasn't the best dad.

He didn't listen to you, Lasher. I slap myself
with my right hand. He constantly wanted his way
and for me to just tag along. I slap myself with my

left hand. I didn't even know he loved me. That he could feel that emotion anymore. But he said it— mouthed it.

I bang and bang on the window. "Ahhhh!" I grab the chair by the wall and ram it against the window again and again. The leg breaks. A scratch forms on the window, but it doesn't break. Why won't it break? Why won't this hospital let me kill myself?

Two nurses rush in. One slides both her arms underneath my armpits and tries to lock my arms back, but I'm fighting with the other nurse pulling at the chair. This tug of war over a chair angers me more, so I let go. She's taken aback by my release and falls onto the floor with the chair in her hand. She holds up her hand at the other nurse, to assure her she's okay. The other nurse continues to hold me in the lock, but I just fall to my knees. My head falls forward. The other nurse stands. I see her blue-and-black sneakers at a distance from me.

The nurse across from me speaks first, breaking the rhythms of our huffing and puffing. "Are you ready for the nurse to release you?"

I don't look at her. I continue to gaze at her shoes. What is my life? I don't respond to her question because I don't know what my anger is capable of.

"Lasher? Can you look at me?"

I don't.

"Are you okay?"

What do you think?

The nurse holding onto me tries to pull me back up, I'm assuming to the bed. but I fight to stay in this spot. To not move at all. A silence falls in the room.

"We just want you to get to a calm state and then move back to the bed," the nurse across from me says.

I look at her finally. Her short brown hair is staticky. She looks young and she's short. I nod once. She nods back and then nods again at the nurse holding me.

The nurse holding me stands me up. This time when she walks me backward, I follow. She releases one of my arms, then helps me sit gently on the bed. She fully lets go of me, but stands at an angle, cautious. I spot a needle in her pocket. That's what I want.

I let both of my hands rest at the rim of the bed, then I start to ball up the sheet into my fists. I then scream again. I yell in her face and then they both pin me down to the bed. The nurse on my left holds my arm with one hand and pulls out a needle with her other one. The nurse on the right is using her elbow and body weight to hold down my shoulder and arm. I continue to scream, but I don't fight them. As the needle goes in, I know I'll knock out. It's the only way I can escape right now.

…

The next day I'm sitting up, the covers over my legs and feet, my gaze on the clouds outside the window. The tall buildings in a distance. The window shows no signs of yesterday. I wish I could show no sign of the past few days. But when I go to the bathroom and look in the mirror, I look awful. Dirty and pale at the same time. The scar from the book is barely visible now. When I lay on my side, it hurts from the bald guy kicking me, but they say nothing is cracked or broken.

I feel like a ghost. I feel numb and cold, even though I have no reason to be anymore. I feel the hairs sticking up on the back of my neck. My body is stiff and anxious. I've lost the energy to speak. Just like my appetite, I can't bring myself to do it.

I look at my hands, turned up, feeling unfamiliar with no handcuffs in sight. I put my right hand to the side of me turned up, and my left-hand stays on my lap. I close my eyes. I let my head rest back, but it drops down. Trying to position myself like my dad's lifeless body. I hear nothing. I just see him, across from me, dead.

My head rises and eyelids slip open when I sense someone come to the doorway. I act as if I was looking out the window the whole time. From the corner of my left eye, I see their blurry silhouette. I don't bother turning fully to her. I know it's Olivia. She does two taps on the door. I shouldn't ignore her.

I turn my head and see her in hospital socks and the gown. Her cheek has a purplish bruise on her chestnut skin. She gives a quick, smile, hesitant. She walks in and goes for the other chair that I didn't wreck. She lets it scrape across the floor as she comes toward me, but it's a soft sound and a short motion before she's facing me and my food cart. A strawberry yogurt, chicken sandwich, and apple juice sit untouched. I avoid her presence by looking toward the right of the window.

She sits silently with me for a few minutes. I almost zone out her presence and get lost on a bird that landed on the roof, but her voice enters the air. "The yogurt is pretty good."

I swallow and look at her. Her eyes are heavy with concern. I nod.

She puts her hands on the bed but doesn't reach for my hands. "You want to tell me what you're thinking?"

I shake my head. I don't want to talk to her, and I feel guilty for that. My words won't solve this situation.

She looks down. "I thought so. I heard you're being silent." She shrugs. "I know I was with you and still can't imagine what you're feeling."

I look down at my hands again. I just tried to reenact my dad's dead body. She doesn't need to be in my mind right now. It's dark and questionable.

She adjusts in her seat. "I just wanted to see you, but if you want me to leave . . ."

I meet her eyes. Great, I'm pushing her away. If she goes, then what becomes of me? I'd truly have nobody that cares about me. My right hand clenches, and I shake my head.

She says, "Okay. I'll stay."

I look back at the window because a tear is trying to blur my vision. I swallow it back down. What's crying going to do? I can hear my dad saying, "Figure out a solution. Crying is a distraction."

She looks out the window with me. I don't deserve her friendship, not after what I put her through. But she's still here. I owe her. He left me with a bigger mess.

The other solution instead of moving, was me getting a job, studying on my own without school. I'd buy a book or live in the library. The other solution, was him getting a job he didn't like. The other solutions involved him alive. The other solutions involved us figuring it out together. Maybe, that's where I always went wrong. I should've gone against him. I should've . . . left. I wouldn't have been a burden to him any longer. I would've been alone by choice. Not a stupid little boy waiting for his father to grow up, to be a better dad.

I swallow down more tears.

"You know, I'm still in shock." She shakes her head. "I don't know. . ." Her voice trails off.

Then she continues, "Lash, please don't kill yourself. I . . . I don't know what managing everything must feel like, but I'm glad you're still here. I'm glad you're alive."

I look at her.

"I'm glad we're alive." She looks at her hands. "I'm here if you need anything or when you feel like talking again." She looks back at me. "But I know you haven't eaten or drank anything in days. Please, try. Please."

I look at the food. I can't bring myself to eat that sandwich. My body has become accustomed to eating when my dad's back. And if he's never coming back, and I have this new . . . life? Choice? What is wrong with my head? What is wrong with me?

Olivia grabs the plate and starts to put it on my lap, but I push it, not even wanting the smell of the sandwich to come closer. It nearly falls off the plate, but she regains control and puts it back on the cart. She slowly grabs the yogurt, but just holds it on the cart and looks at me. I shake my head. She points at the apple juice. That's one thing I do. I do drink even if he's not around. I can drink. I nod. She hands me the juice box, and I take it.

"The yogurt is really good. Is it okay if I have it?"

I nod.

She grabs the spoon and opens it. I watch her take a spoonful. And then another. She smiles at me.

I take the straw off the back of the juice box, using my teeth to rip the plastic, and then poke the straw through the aluminum hole covering. I take a small sip and then another.

She smiles again.

A few minutes later her dad comes knocking at the open door. He's wearing a black knitted hat that is fitted to his head. A brown sweater with faded dusty red type patches, and jeans. He's got black sneakers on. I haven't seen Olivia's dad, Barry, since June of this year. He smiles softly at both of us and says, "Someone's here to see you."

Penny peeps out from behind him. She's Olivia's best friend. I'd sometimes eat lunch with them or we'd hangout after school at the movies or eat at Hal's Steaks. We'd split one cheesesteak with chips because we couldn't afford more. She's in a brown bubble-like coat; her wavy hair is in a ponytail. She plays with her fingers, making them a bridge and letting them fall, remaining intertwined.

Olivia immediately stands, puts the empty yogurt container on the cart, and in seconds is in front of her best friend. They hug. I look at Olivia's dad, feeling awkward, not wanting to interrupt their moment. I take another sip of the apple juice and end up finishing it. I put it on the cart and turn back to see Penny looking at me. To my surprise she comes over and hugs me. The scent of cherry slams my nose.

She says, "I'm glad you're okay."

I blink and am surprised by the sincerity in her voice. I rest my head on her shoulder and slowly let my right hand touch her back. I don't know when's the last time I had a hug. When freshman year ended, and we started summer break?

When she pulls back, she shakes her head. "I can't believe they did that to you." She looks back at Olivia. "Both of you. It must hurt."

I think the pain and bruises are my mask. Without them, it would just be me feeling. Without harm done to me, I'm left to heal my inner self, by myself. I'm too afraid of that.

Chapter 13: Harvey
1988 - FALL

I'm hanging with my boys Kent and Cory in Kent's backyard. I know Kent from the shoe store place I used to work at. I met Cory through Carla and her friends at a party after she graduated. It's crazy how we're all nineteen but living different lives. Carla and Lee are in college going for their degrees. Cory has no plans for college or leaving the city. Kent is taking a gap year to build up his design portfolio to get into a good college. I never thought I'd meet a Black guy wanting to get into the fashion industry to design shoes, clothes, heck, even luggage. Then there's me, didn't finish high school, not going to college anytime soon, but at least I'm working.

"Yo, HP, how's your girl doing?" Kent asks.

I let out a puff and pass the weed to Cory. "Which one?"

Cory laughs and holds out his hand for me to slap. I high five him. "Nice, nice."

Kent shakes his head. "Y'all too much. Who got the time for multiple women?"

Cory coughs a little. "Who got the time for a committed relationship?"

Kent takes a hit next. "I'm not about it."

I laugh. "That's because you helplessly want to find the one."

"What's wrong with that?"

"Live. Stop searching for her."

"Yeah. Let her come to you." Cory uses his hands to bring inwards. "She approaches you."

I take another hit.

Cory looks at his pager and sits up. "I gotta head east."

"Why?" Kent asks.

"Work." Cory stands.

I pass the weed to Cory. "My guy, you still selling?"

"I'm making money."

I shake my head. "Ain't safe."

"It's green like the rest." Cory passes it to Kent.

"Be safe, man," Kent says.

Cory purses his lips out. "Quit worrying. I handle myself." He puts on his cap, covering his basically tan bald head. Sure, he has hair, but it's so thin, so low. He's wearing black sweatpants and a hoodie a size too big for him. He heads to his car. "The spirit of Massachusetts am I right?" he holds up a fake blunt, grinning.

I start choking on the hit I just took 'cause he got me laughing. He's referencing that nonstop annoying commercial that would play. "Go," I cough out.

He chuckles and walks off as I collect myself.

Kent shakes his head and takes a puff, then passes it to me. "What we gonna do about him?"

"I got my own shit to worry about," I say.

Kent nods. "How's Tim-Tim?" He kicks off his white-and-black sneakers and rests back on the outdoor lounge chair.

I chuckle. "Good. Smart ass kid." I take two puffs.

"Good looking and smart. Whew. The world ain't gonna be ready for him."

"You ain't lying." I pass it back for Kent to finish.

Kent and I chill in his yard for another hour, seeing how many cheese balls we can catch in our mouth. Sadly, the grass was winning, but Kent believes in the five second rule.

"I could fall asleep right now," I say out loud. "A clear blue sky, no cloud in sight. The breeze feeling just right, and this other chair the right amount of comfort for my feet. Ah, this is peace."

"Not to be that guy, but don't you have work?"

I throw a cheese ball at him. "Why you had to say something? Always ruining a moment."

"*Psh*, not always. I'm helping you make money."

"Those low-ass tips, stuck-up workers, and weak-ass name for a chain? I'm sick of the place."

"You've been there a year. They don't do some award for that?"

I laugh. "No. I wouldn't say people really care for me."

Kent chuckles.

"The only guy I like, he's a delivery guy, too, so I barely see him. We always picking up orders and then off to houses. Only for trainings do we get to kick it."

"Hey, those mozzarella sticks are slamming."

"You and Tim. I'm gonna make y'all do an eating contest where one of you throw up, so you both stop liking them!"

"You're just salty 'cause they don't have your loaded baked potato."

"They're an appetizer place! They should at least have all popular appetizers."

"Come on, over fried cheese? You trippin'!"

I throw another cheese ball at him as I stand up. "I won by the way. Your punishment is to make me a loaded baked potato."

Kent laughs. "You funny, man. Catch ya later."

. . .

I walk in the house at 12:28 a.m., with Ma following behind me. She slams the door. Uncle Roger and Tim sit on the couch watching TV.

"Just let it out already," I say to her. "Was silent the whole car ride. Now, gonna slam everything. Just say it."

She turns and stares, mouth tight and hand to her hip. She sucks in a breath and then points to Uncle Roger. "Not once has he ever gotten fired from a job. Not once."

I nod.

"No. Look at him. Look at him."

I sigh and turn to Uncle Roger.

Uncle Roger simply says, "Uh-hmm."

Ma shakes her head. "You were fired again! Harvey, damn it!"

My fists are clenched, but I don't say anything. My jaw tightens. She's right. I deserve whatever she's about to say.

She gets in my face. "You Mr. Tough Guy? You gonna fight the whole world to prove something?" She slaps my chest with the back of her right hand. "You gonna give up and waste your life away or get arrested one day? You gonna miss out on your brother's life?" She hits me again. "You gonna leave me?" She grabs my face, it's not as forceful as I thought the grip would be. She looks at me with worry in her eyes. "Why are you so angry?"

I look down.

"What did he do?" Tim asks with a huff. He then looks at me. "What did you do?"

Ma lets go of my face.

"I . . . I ate the guy's pizza. He was saying shit, so I sat down right at his door and ate his pizza in front of his face. He called his dad, and his dad called the cops because I wouldn't move. The son called my job. While he was waiting because I know Kaya put him on hold, he kept saying, 'I'm about to talk to the manager. I'm about to talk to him.' I didn't care."

"Come on," Tim says. He shakes his head and doesn't look at me.

"The cops let me go. I dropped the car back off at Appetizers."

"And got fired," Ma finishes. "Then, you went over Kent's and started talking about going back to that guy's house and fighting him. It's not his fault you got fired. Actions have consequences!"

Uncle Roger shakes his head. "Elaina and I had a nice game going until your friend called, concerned. Now, a peaceful night turned into your mom worrying about her oldest son who was supposed to be working and then come home."

"Harvey . . ." Ma says it softly. "What are you mad about all the time?"

I meet Ma's eyes. "I'm a delivery driver and working retail. Ma, my real friends are off in college. Lee's away, and I'm here and barely even helping you. Kids talk shit like they got me figured out. This is not what I want to do. This is not who I am, and I'm tired of them thinking it is! Nobody is accepting my writing! I wanna be able to finish school. I. Want. To. Go. To. College!"

"You will. God will find a way for you."

"Ma, come on. We don't got no money for that right now."

"Right now. But what about the future? Who said you couldn't go to college? Who said that to you?"

I look down. "No one."

"Uh-hmm. So, start believing you will. Where there's a will, there's a way. You gotta show you're willing."

"I don't want to make you worry about me. That's the last thing I want to do. I try to lie low and not do nothin' crazy, but when someone pisses me off, I just blow up."

Ma shakes her head. She doesn't look at me anymore. She turns and paces, wanting to sit down, but not in dad's chair.

"I still have the retail job," I remind her.

Tim sighs.

I turn to him. "Say it."

Tim shrugs. "You always hid me from Dad's disappointing qualities. You always took care of Mom and me. Why aren't you able to now?"

I shrug. How am I supposed to answer that? Not like I want to be the man of the house.

"It's like Dad's . . ." Tim bites his lip, unsure whether to finish.

I shake my head. "When Dad was here, I knew I wanted to be better than him." I point to myself. "Now I don't know what better is. It keeps feeling like . . ." I throw my arm out. "I was wrong for thinking I was a better person than him."

"You're nothing like him," Tim tells me. "That's why I don't get why . . . it's like you're trying to be! You're better than that, HP. Fuck people. Seriously, fuck them. It's nothing wrong with caring for your family. And there's nothing wrong with Mom and I protecting you. You don't always have to look out for us. Let's just figure it out together, so it's not you against everyone. We're a family."

"Remember your goal. College," Uncle Roger says.

I swallow. My goal. Yeah.

College, writing, workshops, screenplay drafts, internship, writing contest wins, accepted by an agent, an offer, movie.

That goal.

Chapter 14: Lasher
2012 – WINTER

I'm having a session with Ms. Lyn, my new social worker. I only met her two days ago. She seems by the book but a little timid. I can't tell if she's timid to be around kids in my situation or if that's just her. I don't know if this is the right field to be shy in, though.

I'm in a home with other foster kids. We're in one of the offices. I was able to grab two backpacks and two boxes full of my stuff from the apartment. My movies, some clothes, an extra pair of shoes, two pairs of my dad's clothes, and an old shoebox he had of stuff from his childhood. I got my cellphone back, so that's a plus. I can still have that to contact Olivia.

"I think I found a foster family for you. Two parents. Their children just started college."

I don't want to hear this right now. I don't want a new life. I don't want a fake family. "I don't have a family," I tell her.

"Families are not always blood related, Lasher. Some people find their family. Some people get a start over. Some people make their own family. Family is about those who truly care and love you."

"He loved me." I look at her.

She swallows.

"He said . . ." I look down at my lap, sucking on my teeth. *It's my fault.* "He's dead because I doubted him." I look back at her. "I didn't believe in him."

"Lasher, your dad made his own choices. That's not your fault."

I slap myself. I secretly believed he was being stupid and acting like the child. I secretly thought he wasn't doing the right thing and that I could suggest something better. My negativity put us in the situation. I slap myself harder.

"Lasher . . . I'm going to ask you to find another solution instead of slapping yourself when you're upset about your dad or with yourself." She wraps her hand around my left wrist and holds it down.

I slap myself with my right hand.

She grabs that wrist, too, and holds it down. "Lasher, you did nothing wrong."

I look at her grip on me and try to yank my hands up, but she's holding them tight.

"Look at me," she says. "Lasher, please look at me."

I hold in my breath and meet her eyes.

"When you feel this upset with yourself . . . When you start to think it's your fault that your dad died, I want you to count backward from ten."

Come on. Really? I try to yank my arms up again, but she keeps them down.

"Just try it. Try it with me. 10. 9." She tilts her head. "I'm going to restart. I won't be saying the numbers alone. 10."

I let out my breath in her face. "10," I huff.

"9."

"9," I grit through my teeth.

"8."

"8," I breathe out.

"7," we say at the same time.

She nods and forms a short smile at being in sync.

"6. 5. 4. 3. 2. 1."

"Good. That can help recenter your mind. To make it stop having so many rushing thoughts and restart. Instead of thinking about your dad and how you feel about what happened, I want you to think about something that calms you. Something that comforts you no matter where you are."

I purse my lips, tilting my head and tossing my hands out. How am I supposed to figure out what comforts me? "Nothing. I don't know."

"For me, I close my eyes and think of the sound of rushing water. I start with something beautiful like a waterfall." She's smiling wide as she says this. "Then I get smaller and smaller, from the sound of waves at the beach crashing against each other to a nice hot shower. Then I think of a bathtub where you have to let the water fill, and that's comforting for me because when I take a bath I feel better."

I blink, not wanting to picture her in a bath.

"Then, I think about a faucet. The water turned on. I can do hot. I can do cold. I can mix them and then splash my face. Look in the mirror or sit on top of the toilet seat and just close my eyes. And all I hear is that water. The rushing, overpouring sound of it. And the nice thing is, I can find that sound no matter where I am. If I'm out, there's usually a place with a bathroom, which means there's a sink. If I'm in a different country, but staying at a hotel or a friend's place, there's a bathroom. I may need to escape there. And if I'm really lucky and on a vacation, I get to hear it at the beach. Or get my butt out to a hiking trail so I can find a nice waterfall to sit near. But at least I have the sink."

"You're smiling."

She nods and lets out a breath in my face. Her breath smells like watermelon gum. "Yeah. It makes me feel better. Now, it's your turn. Close your eyes, and try to think of something."

I look down, forgetting she was still restricting my wrist. I look back at her and close my eyes. It doesn't feel comfortable, and I still see her silhouette floating in the dark, so I open them again. She nods, encouraging me to close them again. I sigh and close them a second time. I wait for her silhouette to get smaller and smaller and reshaped and then gone. Now it's just the light and weird coloring.

"What is one thing you can think of that makes you smile," she says softly. The watermelon scent is more noticeable this time.

I take a breath, trying to think of something. When I see soda in the fridge? No, that's dumb. When I get to hang out with my friends. "My friends," I mumble.

"That's a great answer. Friends can make us smile and really be there for us. But I want to remind you sometimes friends aren't available. Sometimes friends move."

"I moved," I corrected.

"Exactly. So, while friends are great, they can't always be with you. I want your comfort to not be dependent on a person. Instead, something that can be with you no matter where you are."

Fine. Well, all I can picture is hanging out with my friends. Especially when we'd go out together. Get food. Or even to the movies. Yeah, the movies are alright. We usually watch a comedy. That's not true, fantasy and action, too, but my favorite is comedy. "Movies?" I ask. "I like comedy movies."

"Good. Good."

Her second good, makes it feel like a but is coming. What's the point of asking me if all my answers are wrong? I barely like anything.

"Remember, sometimes movies can be expensive. Do you own a lot of movies?"

"Uh, yeah. Some."

"Okay. Then, I do like that answer."

"You don't sound like you do." I open my eyes.

She finally lets go of my arms. "I love that you took that time to think about things that make you smile. I'm glad you have some comforts."

Three comforts. Boy, what a lot.

"I let go because I could tell you were calmer. It was in your voice, in the way your arms weren't tightened or tensed anymore. And your posture changed from upright to slouch."

"I thought slouching was bad."

"And look, even some humor. But yes, you're right. Slouching isn't good for the back." She adjusts herself to sit up better. "But, Lasher, I want you to remember this technique. Count backward from ten. Close your eyes and think of your comfort."

"You always going to monitor me and stop me from slapping myself?"

"I won't always be here. This is up to you to do. Remember, you have that notebook. Grab a pencil and write. Write to your dad. Write to Olivia. Write to me. Write to no one. Write to yourself."

"I guess." I look out the office window. "I wish I could've been able to talk to him."

She nods. "I'm sorry you weren't able to. But, don't blame yourself for your dad's death. You did what you could. You waited for your dad when he left. You told those guys that your dad was getting the money. That probably gave your dad more time. Your dad hid a lot from you. Your dad made choices, even if they were bad decisions. *He* chose to do them. That's not on you. You wanted to help. You tried to help. But he wouldn't let you. That doesn't mean you're a bad son. You were a good son to him. That, he knew."

She continues, "That's why he chose to save you. He sacrificed his life because that's the choice he made. And he knew you deserved to still be living. Don't forget that choice. Don't forget he wanted you to be okay."

I nod.

The next day, Ms. Lyn tells me it didn't go through with that family. That she'll keep looking. No one wants me though. It's his fault. It's not enough he kept me alive. What about helping me have a future? He hasn't prepared me for anything. He chose for me to live, without helping me survive. All the times I thought about leaving him was when I was younger. I still blamed him for me not having a mom or knowing about my family. Back then people would've taken me in. Now? I'm just a fucked-up teen. That was his choice, too. To make me fucked-up.

A day later, I wake up at 4 a.m. This has become my new routine. Only this morning there's a reason I can't sleep. His funeral is today. I'm not going. Of all people to be handling his funeral, it's his mom. My grandma, Elaina. The same lady that kicked my dad out and isolated him. Ms. Lyn told me Elaina wanted to reach out to me. Look at what happened. She doesn't get to be in my life now. Whoever shows up at his funeral— how much did they really care about my dad? And I'm just supposed to go and have people say "Sorry" to me? Look at me.

I'm in a group home with other parentless kids. It's noisier. I try not to hear their stories. Hear how we're all fucked up. Hear how we got screwed over.

The notebook slides off my chest as I sit up. Day five of journaling. Day five of writing to my dad because I don't see the point in life. The pen has slipped under my thigh. I press myself against the wall, put my feet up on the bar of the bottom of the bunk bed, and rest the notebook on my knees to get as much light coming through the window. I wouldn't harm myself with a pen. I've gone a whole day without slapping myself. Seeing these other kids just makes me mad at life.

I'm fucked up because of you. I loved you. You didn't care about me. What, I'm alive because of you? I wouldn't have been in that situation if it weren't for you. Olivia's life shouldn't have been in your hands. You owe me. You owe me, and you're dead. I don't owe you shit. I don't owe you the satisfaction of believing you had a plan. I don't owe you loyalty and respect. I don't owe you my tears. I don't owe you my pain. I succumbed to you. I followed you. And you still didn't listen to me. I don't owe you my face at your funeral and any words that would show how twisted I am because I'm your son.

I don't owe you a damn thing.

YOU OWE ME. YOU FUCKING OWE ME.

I throw the notebook to the floor. I stare out the window wanting to see something and not feel everything. It's a clear night out, and the moon is shining. It's not full. That's where I want to be right now. Sitting up on the moon. Looking over the world. Seeing what it really has to offer. What I would miss. What I should be fighting for. What it wants from me.

What I want from it. I need an answer. What was my dad trying to prove to this world? What is this world really? Pitiful? A scum? Infinite? Nothing? Existing to bring forth an unknown that may not be anything at all but existence itself?

Why was I born with parents that didn't know how to take care of me?

How do you love a family of one?

You don't. I want to be more than one. I'm tired of feeling lonely. Who wants a fucked-up teen? There's already too many of us in this world. Why try to help another one? Let us suffer, right? What's another day of suffering going to do to us? Nothing. We're used to it, right?

I don't want to be used to it.

I just want someone to want to help me. To want to support me.

I slide down on the bed but take the pillow from behind my head. I press it into my face and the tears pour. I scream into the pillow. I clutch the pillow with all my might, and my whole body shakes out the tears. I need to wring them out of my body. I need to feel something else. Anything better than this.

Chapter 15: Harvey
1988 - FALL

I'm sitting in the backyard smoking when Ma comes and joins me. I cough a little and sit up, surprised she wants to be around the smoke and smell. She's never expressed anything against weed before, but I also don't know what she thinks about me smoking it.

"What's up? You want to talk?" I tap the blunt so the ends fall into my empty soda can before resting it across the mouthpiece.

"No, not really. You can keep smoking. I just wanted to be outside. Sit with you for a moment," she says. She wraps her thicker, brown cardigan around her tighter so she's comfy in the night's air.

"You sure?"

She smiles and turns to me. "You're not the first person that's smoked around me."

"Who else has? Dad?"

She shakes her head. "He wasn't a smoker. Uncle Roger used to be though." She looks out, stares at our grill. "May still do it from time to time. I used to have a friend that did it religiously. Always high."

I pick back up my blunt and relight it. "You ever try it?"

She does a single nod.

"Really?" I take a puff and suck in before blowing it out, to the right of me, away from Ma.

"I cough too much."

I nod and start coughing myself. I hunch over, covering my mouth with my left arm. "You . . . jinxed me," I wheeze. I collect myself and sit back. "That does happen from time to time."

She smirks but shakes her head. "I don't like it."

"We get choked up from crying. Do we like that?"

"There's usually an emotional reason attached to it. There's no emotion attached to smoking weed."

"You sure? I think the mouth that takes the hit is the same mouth that's got a lot of emotion they're holding in." I hold up the blunt. "So, they find an easier release with this, than talking about it."

She looks at me. First with worry, but she then blinks and softens her face. She turns and looks down at her hands to place them in the sleeves of her cardigan.

"Ma, if you're cold, go inside."

"I did come out to ask you one question. Every time you come out here alone, I wonder . . ." She looks up at the stars we can see. "If you're praying sometimes. Not just thinking or letting off steam, but praying."

I take another hit to think about her question. When I blow out, I want to take another hit, but I don't want to keep her out here longer than she needs to be. "No. I'm sorry, Ma. Sometimes I may ask God in certain circumstances to forgive me." I lift a shoulder and look at her. She looks at me. "Like at Dad's funeral I was so mad, but you and Tim were so sad, so I wanted to be respectful. I didn't want to give off some demeanor. So, I asked God to help or forgive me." I shrug. "I did pray for a job one time when things were going downhill. But, I don't pray often. I don't know how I feel . . . about God. Or how to talk to him?"

She nods. "I am glad to hear sometimes a prayer comes out. But, I sadly figured you didn't pray much or at all." She looks down at her lap. "That's the one thing I wish I stood my ground on." She looks at me again with a half smile. "I had wanted you and Tim to go to Catholic schools. I went. I just think you having a Bible class and being around others to have discussion with, wear a uniform, learn some discipline . . . would have been good for yall."

"Really? I never knew. Why didn't you send us?"

"Your father said he grew up believing without going to a school for it. He said y'all needed more of an education around the people without faith, who would challenge y'all. I thought I understood what he meant. But, I think if y'all went to a Catholic school it would've made y'all stronger. Know how to protect yourselves more."

I shrug. "I mean, I don't know. You could've taken us to church more? Or bible study."

She nods. "I could've."

I let the blunt rest between my fingertips and use my other hand to touch her arm. "Hey, Ma, I'll do it for you. My kids will go to a Catholic school."

A smile escapes her before she shakes her head. "I'm not asking you to do that."

"I want to. Heck, I want them to be better than me. If a Catholic school could help that, so be it!"

She smiles again. "I love you."

"I love you too, Ma."

Chapter 16: Lasher
2012 - WINTER

A week later Ms. Lyn finds a couple that will take me in. A couple that lives an hour away from where I'm used to. The Jameses. They seem like an average couple, they only had one child at a young age, and he's in college now. They didn't want to come empty-handed so they give me a gift. A Hersheypark T-shirt. Apparently, they go every year and have a ton of shirts.

"Who doesn't like chocolate?" Mr. James says. We're in the foster care office building.

And when I tell them I've never been, Mrs. James says, "We'll take you. You'll love it. Get all the fudge and hot chocolate you want." Her smile is tight. It looks creepy and uncomfortable, but I think it's her normal smile. Maybe she's nervous?

"Did you and your dad have any family traditions?"

I swallow at the question and shake my head.

Mr. James nods. "That's alright. Always time to start a tradition."

"Not when you don't have a family," I tell him.

He looks at Mrs. James. She rubs his arm as she bites her lip. They don't look back at me and I turn away from them and look out the window.

Ms. Lyn comes around to me. "Lasher, I'm just asking you to try," she says softly.

I stare at a bird pecking at the ground. I don't see any food.

"They'll take care of you. If you really want to move after some time, I'll keep looking." She whispers this to me, her back to the Jameses.

Keep looking for who? My forced family? My made-up family? I'm not their son. I'll never really be their son. They're too late to come and rescue me.

"Okay?" she continues.

I turn to her and actually look at her. Her hair is frizzy and in a brown messy ponytail. She looks tired, wearing gray dress pants with a matching cardigan and a wrinkled royal blue shirt underneath. I used to think she was probably forty-something, but I think she's younger. She has a wide face, sand-tannish skin tone, thin eyebrows and lips, wide eyes. She isn't my problem. She is doing her job. She's trying, and I shouldn't be rude to her. She doesn't deserve my anger. I can't just dump it on her or anyone. The person I should've dumped it on is dead. That's no one's fault but my own. Actually, there are people that could've prevented my trauma and awful upbringing. They're to blame. My dad's mom. My mom. My dad's family. My dad's support group. My school. My neighbors. My friends. My dad. Myself. My fucking self.

"I'll be checking in every week." Ms. Lyn says, giving me an awkward pat to my back.

"Thank you," I tell her.

A smile forms on her lips. That's the comfort she needed.

Twenty minutes later, I'm in a weird green Nissan car. It looks like it's dirty, but that's just its shade. It's so weird it's comforting. It's not puke. It's not ugly. Its existence is just weird. They could have chosen silver, white, black, a red even, but they have this. And an hour and fifteen minutes later I'd rather stay in this car than their house.

This green Nissan pulls into the front of the faded red house that looks like brown brick. They have an open, two-car driveway and a big bush in front of their house on the left. Boring dark brown roof and overhead to match the rustic door. A three-story house with five windows. Their neighbors are about six feet away on both sides. The house just reminds me how distant I am from my life.

When my dad and I lived in a house, it was attached to three other homes. Not much individualized ours besides the white gate, steps going up to our house—not cracking like the others—and our first gated door didn't creak as loud as our neighbors. Instead, it was our main door that you had to force open and lift up to lock close that we had the trouble with. But, that was comforting. We didn't stand out too much and that neighborhood was quiet. Yeah, cars flew by at night, and it got busy when school would end with kids passing through, but really everyone kept to themselves. If someone was sitting on the porch you nodded or said hi. You didn't have to keep a conversation or help or be nosy. You just lived.

This house isn't trying to be discreet. Plus, houses around it are stoned or upgraded. This street differs from house to house, and I know my dad wouldn't want to live on such a "look at me" block. Knowing that, I can't even picture myself accepting it.

"You ready to see the place?" Mr. James asks.

When I don't respond he turns to me and so does Mrs. James. I swallow. How do I say no, politely?

"You okay?" Mrs. James asks.

I'm frozen. They're staring at me, I can hear my heart more. It's thumping and thumping and waiting for me to decide. Waiting for me to hit myself for judging my dad's taste. Or should I hit myself for being rude to the Jameses. They're offering me a place to stay. I'm sure it's warm. I bet it's nice.

My hands tense and fingers curl into my palms. Do I deserve this? Why do I want a dead man's approval? *Why do I wish you were here?* Do I really, or am I more scared that I'm going to screw this up?

Maybe I never would have left him because I feared failing just like him. He made me fail. If I failed due to choices he made, then I had someone to blame. But, if I failed without him, then . . . I'm no better than him. I want to be better than him.

I want to be better than you.

I feel the heat in my palms, the bottoms of my feet, my neck and underarms. Ms. Lyn said not to fall back into those unhealthy habits. She said to count backward from ten. To close my eyes. To find something that makes me happy and think of that. The blurry images of Mr. and Mrs. James fade as I close my eyes. Ten, nine, eight, seven, six, five, four, three, two, one. I let out a breath.

Comedy movies make me happy, but I don't have a favorite. I just like laughing because I didn't do it much with my dad, but I could do it with my friends. Friends, like how Declan used to be. Olivia. Penny? Friends that I barely have and can't see right now. But I can't tie my happiness to others, I have to choose something. Something I can do no matter where I am. I don't know. The only thing that calms me is writing. It feels like I'm talking to someone. Anyone. My dad. Ms. Lyn. The hospital nurses. Olivia. Another world.

The notebooks with the punched holes. The rings. The ones without the tearable dashes. I can't stand the tearable sheets. I love ripping the notebooks and leaving fragments of the paper sticking every which way and looking frazzle. That's my comfort. It can be so neat and teared away so dejected.

I open my eyes and I see Mr. James is no longer in the car. Mrs. James reaches her hand to pat my knee. "Are you okay? Ms. Lyn told us you have been practicing breathing techniques when you're overwhelmed. I told Neal I think you're just trying to adjust the best you can."

I blink, surprised Mr. James's name is Neal. A Black man with a boxy head and stature, looking like a mix of a high school teacher and a guard that stands in front of a club; and his name is Neal. And she looks like a mixed Black woman, I'm not sure though, curly brown hair to her shoulders, wearing jewelry galore on her neck, wrists, and earrings.

I nod. "Yes." My voice is back. That calming down method worked. I unclench my hands and roll my ankle around to loosen it. I look at the house again. I might as well see the inside.

Chapter 17: Harvey
1989 - SPRING

I'm already twenty. Not a teen anymore. I honestly try to shake my temper. I listen to music at work to not hear people's smart comments or nonsense small talk. I watch the show *Cops* when I know I'm missing hanging out with friends. I watch *A Different World* for hope for my future and to get my mind off my reality. I'm pushing down my temper the best way I can.

Plus, I joined a local writing workshop that meets Saturday mornings. Most of the people are adults, probably in their forties or fifties, but there's one person in their thirties. I'm the only Black male, and there's one older Black lady. But, I still feel the feedback I receive on my writing is genuine. It's helpful getting others input. Plus, it's cool hearing other genres. The group mainly writes fantasy or romance. One person writes historical fiction.

It's springtime, where the excitement of the weather being in the high sixties makes things peaceful. Before the heat, humidity, sweat stains, and breaking out the fans that make me wish spring lasted longer. I'm driving Tim back home from his girlfriend's house.

"No. Tell me again what you said?" I'm cracking up.

"Stop. You're just laughing at me."

"You right. I am."

Tim shakes his head. "I said . . . 'Great, Scotts' like Doc in the movie."

I stop at the red light and bang my hand on the wheel. "I can't believe you said that to her. She's shirtless . . . and you say . . . Ah, that's too funny." I turn on my right turn signal.

Tim laughs a little but slaps my shoulder. "Shut up."

I start turning as the light for the other traffic turns red. Then I stop as the light takes a second longer to turn green than I expected. When it finally turns green, I make a complete right turn. After a moment we hear a cop car behind us.

Tim turns. "Is that for us?"

I sigh and pull over. "Fuck. Let's see." I watch as the cop car pulls over too. An officer steps out of the car. "You okay?" I look at Tim.

He nods.

The officer stands at my already rolled down window. He's got a haircut that looks uneven on his small head, and ugly stubble that you can tell would look better if he had a full beard. "Sir, do you know why I pulled you over?" his voice sounding nasally and monotone.

I shake my head. "No, I don't."

"You turned on a red light."

I meet the officer's eyes. "No. No, I didn't."

"I watched you."

"He didn't, officer. He waited 'til it was green," Tim says.

"Can I see some ID?" the officer puts a hand to his hip.

I announce, "I'm grabbing my wallet from my pocket." I slide out my wallet, keeping my left hand up in sight for the officer.

Tim keeps his hands on his lap.

The officer takes my ID and then says, "Both of you."

Me and Tim both look at him. "You don't need anything from him. I was driving. He's just sitting there."

"Both ID's."

"I-I only have a student ID," Tim answers.

In a stern tone he demands, "Let me see." Then questions, "How old are you?"

"Seventeen," Tim stammers. Tim digs in his backpack in front of him. "I'm getting it." He carefully slides out his ID. "H-Here." He reaches past my face to put it in the officer's stretched out hand.

The officer makes a *tsk* sound. He looks at both of us for a moment before walking back to the cop car.

I grip the wheel tight. "Why? Why today?"

"Just listen and keep cool."

"Gonna tell me I ran a red light? I waited."

"You turned a little, but you didn't go all the way 'til it was green," Tim says.

I turn to him. "You're saying I turned on a red light?"

"No. No, HP. I'm saying the slightest turn of your wheels is his excuse to say you did wrong. They got nothing better to do sometimes."

I inhale and exhale. Inhale and exhale.

The officer comes back. "Here."

I take my ID and put it back in my wallet and hand Tim his. "Can I go?" I ask.

"I'm gonna need you to step out the vehicle."

I shake my head. *Come on.* "What for?"

"Step out."

"What for?" I repeat.

I glance at Tim who's looking out his window. Unbelievable. That officer came back and brought his partner to the car, too.

"You're disobeying orders. Don't make me ask you again."

The second officer knocks on Tim's window with his knuckle.

I look back and forth between these officers.

"Officer, you said this was over a red light. Just give us a ticket," Tim says.

"I want to search the vehicle," the officer demands.

"You don't have a right to do this." I furl my eyebrows and look at him.

The officer starts leaning in the car to grab me.

"Don't touch me," I yell. Fuck no. I slap the officer's hand. "Back up. Don't put your hands on me."

"Get out the car. I have suspicion to believe—"

"This isn't necessary. We didn't do anything," Tim says. He looks back and forth between officers.

"Get out the car," the second officer says. He starts yanking at the door handle.

The officer on my side has the audacity to look at me, snarling, like he's going to reach his arm over the window to open the door himself.

Tim sighs and unbuckles his seatbelt, He unlocks the door and gets out the car. He places his hands on the hood of the car. The second officer starts patting him down. He's taller than his partner but looks younger, with a wide face.

I throw my seatbelt off and open the door, intentionally bumping the officer. I place my hands on the car near the back seats. The first officer pats me down with force against my legs, hips, back, and sides. I look at Tim.

"Clean," the second officer announces to his partner about Tim. He then starts tapping his foot. Is he the one bothered?

The first officer forces me over so that we're facing, slamming me against the car.

"Come on, man." I push him.

I hear the second officer tell Tim to put his hands back on the car.

"Hands up." The first officer orders me. I smell coffee on his breath.

I poke the inside of my mouth. Really being tested today. My chest rises and falls. I slowly raise my hands.

The first officer pats me down and finds nothing.

"Let us go. This ain't right, and you know it," I tell them.

"Hands on the car." He doesn't meet my eyes.

I turn back around and look at Tim. "You alright?"

Tim nods, hunched over on the hood of the car, waiting. Biting his lip and glancing back at the second officer.

The second officer holds out a taser. Looking at the back of Tim and watching me.

"You're under arrest," I hear the first officer say behind me. He grabs my arms before I have time to process. My face and chest hit onto the car. He places handcuffs on me.

"What? What for?!" Tim and I ask.

"For possession," the first officer says.

"You're full of shit! Possession of what?" I spit.

Tim talks to the second officer. "Don't do this. Just give us a freaking ticket."

"Possession of what?" I turn and get in his face now, making him look me in the eyes. Until I hear a bang against the car from behind me. I turn around.

"Tim? Tim?" He's nowhere in sight anymore. I start moving to the front of the car. I see Tim's gray-and-white sneakers.

"Get up." The second officer kicks Tim's legs.

I tug out the first officer's grip and get around the car. I see blood spilling from Tim's head. "What did you do?" My lips are trembling. I fall to my knees. "Tim." There's blood on the edge of my front light.

The first officer pulls me back up. He drags me to the police car.

"Help him!" I yell.

The second officer bends down. He speaks into his walkie-talkie.

I yank my body left, then right, trying to get this officer off me. It's his fault. He'll pay. The officer shoves me to the ground, turns me over, and punches me. "Stay down," he demands. I hear another cop car arrive as another punch hits my face.

Chapter 18: Lasher
2012 - WINTER

I've been here two weeks. The house is unexpectedly tight on the inside. For a modern home, there's so much wood. The living room has a light gray wall and hardwood floors. There's this burgundy, old-style couch, with an old-fashion, grandma-like rug that spreads under the couch, coffee table, and TV. It's humongous and might as well be the floor. The kitchen is spacious, though. I'm in my first home with an island, but the wood floors, cabinets, and island countertop give it a bland vibe. The silver fridge and freezer save it at least. Yet, when the sun comes in on it all, it looks natural.

They have an office area that doubles as storage of their son's things. They have a half bath that is normal. Actually, that bathroom and the bathroom upstairs are manageable. It's a whitish color and sure, the floor is hardwood, but that's where the brown stops. The cabinets are black, and the sink and countertop are white. There's a door that goes downstairs to a basement, but I never wanted to go down and see it. Their second floor is all the bedrooms. They have a tan carpet in their room, a brown bedframe, and whitish walls. The rest of the bedrooms have hardwood floors.

The room I stay in has white walls, a bedframe, and a wooden desk like their son was in college while at home. There's a corkboard and a mirror on the back of the closet. Other than that, it's an empty room. It's not my home. It's not my comfort. It's not a place I want to get used to.

I have to live an hour and some change away from the area I know. It makes it hard to see Olivia. I don't want this. Ms. Lyn was wrong. This is not best. This is taking me from any type of normal. How the fuck am I supposed to be okay if I'm kept away from everything and everyone I know? Am I gonna start school around here? Fuck.

I stayed in this room the whole day. I tried to write and couldn't. I tried to watch one of my comedy movies, but I ended up looking at it on mute like how my dad watched TV shows. But then, I stopped paying attention to it. It's unreal that I'm in this situation.

My phone rings, and I'm surprised of the area code. 540. The only reason I know this call is from Fredericksburg, Virginia is because Declan used to correct me all the time for saying 450. I answer on the fourth buzz. "H-Hello?"

"Is this Lasher?"

"Who is this?"

"Declan. I'm calling for Lasher."

I shake my head and walk to the window. I lean against the window frame, the chill against my arm reminds me this is real. "Hey. This is Lasher. Wow. How'd you get my number?" I haven't spoken to Declan since we were like thirteen. We tried staying in touch after our dad's left anger management, but quickly, my dad started distancing himself. He seemed to be battling with his improved version of himself and the fact that he had to get help. It's like he wanted to forget the guys that went through it with him, even though it made him better. I felt like I was betraying him when I would tell him I had talked to Declan, so I started to talk to him less and less. Then, when my dad and I moved back to Pennsylvania, it felt like the connection completely fell off. I never wanted it to, though.

"At the funeral. I asked around and met a lady, and she gave it to me."

What lady had my number? Could Ms. Lyn have gone? I guess that's nice of her. Wait, he just said at the funeral. "You were here?"

"Yeah. You know our dads were close. Sadly, it was last minute so not many of the other guys could go."

"Yeah."

"My dad and I were at the funeral and . . . shocked we didn't see you."

I don't say anything. Do they know how he died?

"I'm sorry, Lasher," he says.

"Thanks," I say.

"We should've kept in contact."

I scratch my head. "Yeah. That's all I wanted."

"Your dad didn't jump on the idea to hit the road and see—"

I stop him. "No. No. He . . . he didn't. He didn't feel he was ready to see y'all. He wanted to be in a better place. I don't think he ever knew that he was pushing better places away. That's why he's dead. And he never listened to me! He never wanted to hear anything but his damn inner monologues."

Now Declan is the one to stay silent.

I walk over to the bed and tug at the ends of my hair. "Sorry. I . . ."

"In the back of my mind, I feared you didn't show because you were hiding massive bruises he gave you," he says.

In a way I do. These bruises are because he left me to be kidnapped.

"I don't know if you heard about Hank," he says. "His wife divorced him, and he got worse. He's in jail."

"Declan, I was kidnapped." I chuckle at the profound, disbelief of it all. "He got into money trouble that almost killed me, too." I shake my head. "I don't know what to think."

"That's messed up."

I breathe out a "Yeah."

"You get hurt?"

"Bruises. Mostly on my sides."

He's silent.

"The worst part is my friend was kidnapped, too. Wasn't even supposed to be caught in the mix."

"Damn."

"We're both alive. He's dead. I'm just . . . angry."

"Ironic," he says.

"When we were kids, I feared feeling angry. I didn't want to turn out like them. But anger . . . it's not always physical. Anger can be pure emotion too."

"Yeah. That's something those little guidebooks didn't tell us. Just telling us to share how we feel, not be scared of the temper. What about if we feel the temper? What are we supposed to do when we can't talk about it? They never knew what to do with us. You know what I turned to?"

"Drinking?" I suppose.

He chuckles. "No. Wrestling."

"Not for me."

"So, you drink?"

I chuckle now. "No. I hold it in."

"That's not good, man."

"Yeah," is all I can say.

"So, uh, because we all couldn't make it to the funeral, the whole gang planned a short trip to go back to Pennsylvania because we wanted to . . . check on you."

"Oh. That's uh, nice." The whole gang as in the guys from the anger management group. I wonder if their coach is included, too.

"We're uh, here now. For two days."

I swallow. "Now?"

"Yeah."

I shake my head. "That's uh . . . wow." To see them? See Declan again? "My situation is . . . a mess."

"Lasher, we're not here to judge. We just want to check in."

"Where are y'all even at?"

He's in the Woodpin area. It's not too far from where my dad and I used to live. Though it's an hour away from here, it's worth it.

"Can we meet tonight?"

"Tonight?" he says surprised. "I mean we thought . . . grab food or something during the d—"

"You're here. Why waste more time?" Maybe this is what I need to stop being in my head about the past. "I'll meet near there and call you at a spot you can pick me up. Okay?"

"Sure. Okay." He hangs up.

I don't want Mr. or Mrs. James going with me. They'd be there as a sad fog. Following me like an annoying child because they'd know no one else. They really know nothing about my dad. Sure, Ms. Lyn gave them the rundown of the kidnapping situation, but that's that one perspective. He's the villain in their eyes and not my dad. They don't get to be mad and disgusted with a man they didn't even know. They don't get to hear stories about him. I'm the only one that gets to be angry with him.

I unpack one of my bags and throw in sweats, an extra shirt, and my notebook.

I sneak downstairs. Mrs. James must be in the bathroom. She's nowhere in sight, and I hear Mr. James in the kitchen. This is a good time to go. The fifty that my dad didn't take, I've been using it to buy snacks or sodas. I also use some of the change to take the bus, without the Jameses knowing. I usually just go see Olivia or the apartment.

Looking at the route, I could walk some distances so I'm not spending too much of my money. Then I would be good for two bus rides there and two bus rides back tomorrow.

I walk ten minutes to get to the bus that I'll be on for about twenty-five minutes. I forgot how cold it was out here. My hands are already feeling it three minutes in. I have to wait an extra five minutes once I get to the stop for the bus to arrive, but luckily, it's pretty empty. There's only a couple, a man with a cane, a lady, and a guy in the back of the bus.

I sit in the middle, a two-seater near the window, right in front of the blocker that separates the seats from the back door. Sadly, whenever the bus stops and opens for a person in the front, the driver opens it in the back if someone is coming off. So, I feel the cold air every four minutes or so.

I have to wait for another bus, which will be a forty-minute ride. That still doesn't drop me off at their hotel. But when I get off, I can call Declan to pick me up because I'd be about fifteen minutes away.

When I'm a few stops away, I call Declan to ask him to meet me at the bus stop. He asks why I didn't let them pick me up, but I tell him it would've been a hassle.

I'm shivering in the bus stop little cubicle. Both my hands in my pockets. I'm trying not to feel this thirty-degree weather and not think about the basement. It's a little after 8 p.m. now. Finally, Declan and his dad pull up. Declan rolls down the passanger-side window and says, "You look the same. Just with a bigger head."

I crack a smile at that, and I get in the back. I buckle my seatbelt as his dad starts the car.

"Lasher Patts. Boy, it's been some time." His dad, Donnie, looks at me through the rear mirror. "You okay?"

I shrug. "Yeah." I shrug again and blow on my hands to see if that will actually work. "I mean I don't know. How are you guys?"

Declan turns to me. "Yosemite Sam grounded me for smoking."

I bust out laughing. I forgot I said that his dad looked like that when we were younger. Declan wouldn't stop calling him that. Plus, the counselor that worked with all the kids told his dad it's a way Declan was coping. "Maybe that's the way he saw you, and it's up to you to change that." Donnie couldn't get upset around the counselor. But he knew we just thought it was funny, so we kept saying it.

"I didn't blow my cap for nothing," Donnie plays along. "Why would I let you destroy your lungs and body like that? I didn't change my life for you so that you can destroy yours."

Luckily, he still seems to have a good sense of humor about it.

"I thought that's what parenting was all about, letting me experiment?" Declan jokes.

"You still got the beard and all," I comment, looking at his dad's reddish brown hair from the side angle.

"And his big head. Remember your dad used to always say if I were Black and you were white, looks-wise, it was as if we should switch dads." Declan chuckles.

"I do remember that." I look out the window as we stop at a red light.

Donnie glances at me. I don't turn to him. He looks back at the road and there's a silence in the car. We move again when the light switches to green. Silent the rest of the seven minutes.

It's fucking dumb. Dad's not here to enjoy their presence. They all showed up for him. Would he have even done the same? No. He fucking would've been sad he didn't see one of them sooner and hate himself even more. He would have gave himself another reason to be miserable. I realize it now, and I can't help but shake my head. That stupid saying, "misery loves company." I was his company. Or did he just make me miserable like him?

We park in the hotel parking lot. When Donnie shuts the car off, he turns to me again. "Lasher, we're really sorry about Harvey. I wish we could've seen both of you years ago."

I pull at my fingers and nod. I wish that, too.

He grabs my knee and shakes it gently. "How are you holding up, seriously?"

I look at him. For a second, I wish I had just stayed with them when I was younger. For a second, I see who my dad could've been. I swallow. "I'm fucking mad."

He lets go of my knee. "Yeah." He sighs and faces the hotel, grabbing the steering wheel. "Yeah."

Declan doesn't look at me but says, "Your dad lost control again, didn't he?"

"Yeah." They wait for me to explain.

"It wasn't until this year. He actually did fine all these years with his temper. But he always gambled off and on. He actually was doing better until . . . life and losing his job." I let out a breath. "Gambling. I don't know. He wouldn't fucking listen to me."

"Why didn't you go to his funeral?" his dad asks.

I suck in a breath. "Because everything I should have said, I never said to him. Because I feel sorry for me, and I don't need anybody else to. Because I would've broken everything in sight." I pause and look at the car parked next to us. They have a dog stuffed animal sitting in the back, laying in front of the back window. "Because I don't know if I loved him or hated him."

"Why can't it be both?" Donnie asks.

I look at him, though he doesn't look at me. His grip just tightens on the wheel. "Because I've spent this part of my life loving him. I may spend his death hating him."

Donnie let's out a breath. "Whew. That hurts me, Lasher." He looks at me now. "That hurts."

I shrug. Maybe I shouldn't have come. Of course, we'd get real. They know him. They knew who he was before and after. They just didn't know who he was up until . . . They don't see the full picture still. I ball my fist and hit the back of Declan's seat. I throw my head back and close my eyes. My chest keeps rising and falling. I'm fucking angry. Is this what he wanted? For me to become

mad like him. I don't want the anger. I don't want
any part of him. I just want a good life. I want a life I
want to live for. I squeeze my eyes tighter, feeling
my forehead scrunch as I try to take deep breaths
and calm down, but it's not working. I'm just giving
myself a headache. Then a tear squeezes down my
cheek.

"Anger is meant to be felt," Declan says.
"It's not bad to be angry."

"It's what you do with that anger," his dad
finishes.

I let out a breath and snot escapes my nose. I
suck in another breath and release. "I'm nothing like
him." I open my eyes and another tear escapes. "But
I don't know who I am. I literally don't know."

Donnie turns to me and hangs onto my knee.
They both sit in the silence as I try to collect my
tears, my pain, my thoughts, my anger, my dad's
death.

That night was the worst and best night of
my life. I was hugged so many times I almost forgot
it was foreign to me. Almost all the guys were there.
Five others. We sat in Declan and his dad's hotel
room, and they told me how they've been. They
shared memories from anger management days, and
we ordered pizza. I felt like a little kid reunited with

family after going to a school far away from home for way too long. Is this what a family reunion feels like? I didn't want to leave, so I didn't. I told Declan and Donnie I wanted to hangout all day tomorrow. They came to see me, and I want to see them. Donnie agreed I could stay in their hotel room tonight, and him and Declan could share a bed. But, he told me he had to be able to drive me back to wherever I was staying. I agreed.

Chapter 19: Harvey
1989 - SUMMER

Two months later, I sit, waiting for Ma to meet me in the visiting area. It'll be the first time I've seen her since being arrested. The doors open and an officer follows behind Ma. She doesn't have a hair piece; she wears her short hair combed down onto her head flatly. She's wearing a long jean blue dress. Her eyes are heavy. She takes her time to get to me.

I stand. "Ma. Where's your cane?"

She looks me up and down. Noticing my tangled hair, growing fuzz on my face, and apprehensive eyes on her. She's silent for too long. But as she sits, she says, "I left it."

I sit down across from her. "Ma, I missed you."

Ma hugs herself and looks around. At the white walls, at the officers standing in the corners of each table, at the mother to the right of us. When she finally looks in my direction, tears crystallize in her eyes. She sucks in her lips, not looking at my face but at the uniform I'm wearing.

"Ma. Please look at me."

She takes a deep breath before meeting my eyes.

"Is Tim okay?"

A tear slides down her cheek. She wipes it and another falls. Her nails are clear of paint and growth.

I intwine my fingers and rest them on the table. I look down. *Please don't let him be dead. Don't take his life like that,* I pray.

We sit in silence for minutes. I keep my head bowed as Ma continues to cry. The only sound between us are her sniffles. I hear each swallow I'm taking. Please help my Ma. Please stop her tears. Oh, please make her say something. I need her to tell me Tim is okay.

I finally hear a painful, "I told you to stop with the violence."

I look at her now. "Ma—"

She raises her hand to pause me. "I told you to do right. I told you I wanted to see Tim graduate." Her voice cracks. "I told you to protect your brother."

I don't know what to say. I move my hands under the table. I pull at each of my fingers and look down. I've been biting and picking at them so much, they've been bleeding. It should've been me. Not Tim.

"No. You look at me when I talk to you."

I feel heat take over my body. I look at her and tears form in my eyes.

"Tim . . ." she shakes her head. "Tim has some brain damage. Processing difficulty. Speech impairment." She sniffs. "He's not the same person." She puts her hand to her mouth. "I can't imagine . . . I can't imagine what happened. But I know that should've never happened to him. He shouldn't have ended up in the hospital."

Tears fall from my eyes.

"I shouldn't have one boy fighting for his memory and one boy in jail. Not my sons!" she yells louder, pointing in the middle of her chest, "Not my sons!"

I wipe my eyes. She doesn't need to see my tears right now. I sniff and shake my head. There's not one day that goes by that I don't replay that day. I should've been watching Tim, not arguing with that officer.

Ma leans her elbows on the table and puts her forehead in her hands. She cries. Her shoulders and arms curl inwards.

I want to touch her. To hold her.

When she looks back at me, she has to catch her breath. "I can't come back here. I won't come back here."

What? "Ma, please. I never wanted this to happen."

She wipes her face with her hand. "What did happen?"

"Ma, they just plotted on us. Went from saying I turned on red to saying they found us in possession with nothing. There weren't any drugs in my car, Ma. No weapon. Then one was putting handcuffs on me. The other one pushed Tim or something! I feared he had shot him. I don't know why. Tim didn't do nothing." I shake my head. "It's bullshit they both saying self-defense. Tim didn't attack anyone."

"Did you?"

I sniff. "I wanted him off me. I didn't try nothing; I was just pushing him off me."

Ma shakes her head and looks down.

"I didn't do nothing wrong. They just . . . they targeted us, Ma. For no reason."

Ma puts a hand to her mouth, and she looks at me. "I can't get you out. I don't have the money. Uncle Roger doesn't have it. We're praying they drop the charges but they're believing those cops." She looks up at the ceiling. "Why are you testing him? You ain't got no right." She looks back at me shaking her head. "Your father's not playing fair."

"What's he got to do with this?" My hands slide on the table.

"Everything. All of this." She sniffs. "I can't come back here, Harvey." She says it again.

I blink. "What? Ma?"

"I can—"

"You think I did this? You blame me?"

"I'm not saying that."

"You're implying something."

"Evil follows you. Anger follows you. Your father will do whatever it takes to make us stuck. Our marriage was miserable because we both stopped each other from our big breaks."

I shake my head. "What are you talking about?" Why the fuck is she bringing up that man? Why is she telling me this now?

"I gotta do what's best for me, Harvey."

I slam my hand on the table. "You stayed with him!"

She stands, only her fingertips rest on the table. "I see parts of your father in you."

"I'm not him, though!" What is wrong with her? We have the same DNA, of course something is going to stick. But I'm nothing like that man! She raised me to be better than him. How is she going to compare me to him? No fucking way!

She starts to walk away.

"Ma! I'm better than him. Don't treat me like him!" I stand up. "Any part of him you see is because you kept telling me and so I started to believe it." I slam my hand on the table again. "I'll work on the anger. Ma! Ma, come back! Don't do this!" I'm yelling after her as she gets closer and closer to the door. "I'm not him! Ma!"

She walks through the doors, not looking back.

Chapter 20: Lasher
2012 - WINTER

Ms. Lyn is over at the Jameses house.

"We are not sure we can provide Lasher what he needs," Mr. James says.

"Why do you feel this way?" Ms. Lyn asks.

"He doesn't eat with us, barely talks to us, and snuck out more this past week than my son ever did," he says.

Mrs. James continues, "We're not connecting. We want to, and we've given him space to talk when he's comfortable, but he clearly doesn't want to be here."

"Is this true, Lasher?" Ms. Lyn asks, turning to me. We're in the kitchen, a place I rarely go to.

I shrug in the moment. "Yes, but . . . I don't know if it's true."

"You know it's true. You've been sneaking out! Not just to Olivia's." Mr. James's voice rises.

"Not that part," I sigh. "I don't know if I do or don't want to be here."

They all fall silent.

It's not even the suicidal side of me talking. It's the side that doesn't even know who I am and what I want.

Privately, in the living room, Ms. Lyn lays out the alternatives if I don't make it work with the Jameses. I know I don't want that.

So, the next day I tell the Jameses, Olivia and my plan to hangout and watch a movie, since her dad's letting her have an extended winter break into February until she has her first therapy session. They ask what we're going to watch, and I tell them we usually watch comedy movies together.

Mrs. James sits up on the couch. "Have you heard of *Meet the Spartans*?"

I shake my head.

"We saw it in theaters and loved it. Weren't we laughing in the theater?" She lets her hand tap Mr. James's arm.

He nods. "Yep. Liked it so much we bought the DVD."

"You and Olivia should watch it. Let us know if you find it funny, too."

I want to show I'm trying. "Uh, sure. Okay." Hopefully it's funny and I'll be able to give solid feedback.

I'm standing there awkwardly in front of them. It feels like the moment when the teen is asking their parents to go to a party. But, I'm just trying to see my friend and relax.

"I think it's in our room, hun. Get it for him," Mrs. James says.

I force myself to ask them to drive me to Olivia's. To keep them, I have to include them in the things I want to do. But I don't know how to talk to the Jameses. During the car ride the only question I can think of asking is, "how's work going for you guys?" But they're not even working today.

"How long have you and Olivia been friends?" Mr. James's asks.

"Technically, since like 2001."

A silence fills the car, and I realize I should give more detail, but I don't know how to do that and spare the details about my mom lying about my dad's death. I don't want them to look at each other and give the expression through their eyes "no wonder he's messed up."

Finally, Mrs. James asks, "What did you like doing after school? Any sports or activities?"

"No. Just going to the movies, hanging with friends, usual stuff."

This is the most conversation we've had in a day. It feels forced and awkward. It feels like I'm bad at socializing. Bad at doing small talk. I can't even function normally. I'm going to be judged the rest of my life. I'm not gonna make any more friends. I won't have anyone else that'll want to take me in because they'll find me weird or odd. If I lose the Jameses, there's no hope for me.

Finally at Olivia's house and away from the Jameses, I tell her we're watching *Meet The Spartans*. Olivia hasn't heard of it before, but she is down to try it.

I hear the first joke in the movie and then it hits me. I'm watching a comedy movie. I'm trying to laugh right now and he's dead. I can't even remember what his laugh sounds like. He didn't enjoy comedy movies. He barely enjoyed TV. Game shows were his thing more. Trivia. Anything he could manage watching in silence, where questions popped up or the visual was enough.

"Can we mute it?" I blurt out.

I look at Olivia and tune in to hear her say, "What?"

"Can we mute it?" I repeat.

"Uh, yeah. Okay." She half stands, her left leg still bent on the couch. She looks at me and bites the side of her lip. She then fully stands, forgetting where the remote is. She is halfway at the TV when she turns and sees the remote on the arm of the couch on her side. She grabs it and presses the mute button.

I stare at the TV, the colors of their wardrobe, the way their mouth moves and how I don't know what they're saying. I can try to guess. Why did my dad really like doing this?

I feel Olivia's eyes on me. She wants to question my decision or ask me if I'm alright. But she doesn't. She looks back at the screen and adjusts both her legs on the couch. I move to the edge of the couch and look at each character, the way they yell, they walk, the lighting on them, the fighting. I feel like a director. I find myself laughing at their reactions. This is thrilling. Maybe my dad felt more connected to things this way.

But the movie is interrupted when we hear a knock at the door. Olivia and I both turn. She calls for her dad. She fears opening doors because of the kidnapping. I hope her therapist helps her through that.

"Dad," she calls again.

Someone rings the doorbell this time.

Her dad, Barry, comes running down the steps.

"Someone's at the door," she tells him.

We watch as her dad opens the door to a man. He's wearing a black knitted hat and a brown sweater under a peacoat. His black pants look like work pants, similar to Dickies. Pockets on the sides.

He looks older than Olivia's dad. Olivia said family had been calling her to hear how she was doing since the kidnapping. Maybe some are visiting.

Except, he says, "Lasher's my great-nephew and I just wanted to meet him."

Olivia turns to me, but I look at Olivia's dad to see if he believes him.

"Um, how am I supposed to believe that?" Olivia's dad asks the man.

"Harvey's mom is my sister," the man says. He pulls what I guess is his ID out to show Barry. "He left her as his emergency contact. When Elaina was told he died . . ." He trails off. "Harvey left Lasher's number with us, but . . ." He sighs and tries to start again. "When she knew Lasher didn't want communication at the funeral, she didn't want to force herself into his life. But, we wanted to check on him. I just want to see him."

He's family? I look down and realize I'm standing.

Barry says, "I don't know if now is a good time."

"I want to meet him," I say. I stare at the man.

Olivia's dad steps back. The man removes his hat as he walks in. He looks me up and down, puzzled. "Boy," he *tsks*. "Ya got his features. His stance. Different eyes." He has something in his hands.

I swallow. "You were my dad's uncle?" I'm trying to see any resemblance of my dad or him being related to us at all. His eyes maybe? His shade of brown? No. He's not really my dad's uncle. "What's your name?"

"Uncle Roger."

"You were my dad's uncle?"

"Yes," he says.

"When's the last time you saw him?"

He makes another *tsk* sound. "Gosh, might've been . . . close to ten years ago. Before his brother died. He disappeared after that."

"He was getting his life on track."

"I'm glad."

"Until this year."

Uncle Roger shakes his head. "Life got to him."

Barry says, "You can sit or . . ."

Uncle Roger comes over to Olivia and I. Olivia gets up and stands near her dad, so he can sit where she was. I remain standing as Uncle Roger sits. "Did you know about me?"

He tilts his head and sighs. He looks at me. "Kinda. I mean yes. At first, I thought Harvey lost you to your mother. Then—"

"My mom left us."

"I'm sorry," he says. He looks down.

"You said Elaina . . . my dad's mom . . ."

"Oh . . ." He looks at me but then back down, "Yeah . . ." Uncle Roger sighs. ". . . their relationship faltered. Elaina . . ."

"Kicked him out. Gave up."

Uncle Roger swallows. "I don't know if I'd put it that way."

"Why are you here?" My voice rises.

"To check on you." He stays calm. "I heard about the kidnapping." He sits back and clears his throat.

"The kidnapping or his death?"

"The kidnapping. Harvey called Elaina and asked for the money to get you out the situation."

I shake my head. "What do you mean?"

"She didn't have all of it, so I put some money down, too. Harvey said your life depended on it."

Olivia gasps. "He actually got the money back?"

"You're lying," I say. "I found a letter she wrote to him. They weren't on speaking terms!"

He looks at me again. "When you feel death's about to come, sometimes you do the hard things."

I shake my head. He called her? He really did get the money?

"Thank you," Olivia's dad says. But his mouth slides to the side, unsure if that was the right thing to say.

"I want to help," Uncle Roger says into the silence. "I don't want you going from the Jameses house to possibly another foster home if you don't have to."

"What do you mean?" Olivia says for me.

Uncle Roger looks from Olivia to me. "You're family. I want to take you in."

I blink and then look at the floor. I pinch the back of my hair. Suddenly someone wants to show up. Suddenly someone cares.

"I saw the Jameses before coming here because I thought you were there. They made it sound like you were having difficulty. And I've got a stable home. Especially since the girls are grown, so it's just me and my wife."

I can't bring myself to look at him.

"Have you talked to a lawyer or someone about this?" Olivia's dad asks.

"Yes. Before I came here, I wanted to know if it was possible."

"Harvey asked you to take Lasher in?" Olivia asks.

"No. This is me and kinda Elaina, too."

They're asking all the right questions, but it's too late. My dad's dead. The damage they left us to figure out for ourselves has already been laid.

"Where do you live?" Barry asks.

I look up now. Uncle Roger answers, "Massachusetts."

Olivia's eyes widen. "Massachusetts?" she repeats as she looks at me.

I look back at Uncle Roger. "I don't know you."

"We can get to know each other. I know this must be hard for you—"

I shake my head. "You don't know. You don't know what I've been through."

"You're right. I only know what your dad's been through. I know what and who he lost. I've only seen his pain, anger, and actions."

"Not all of it," I snap.

He sucks in his lips. "I don't know how to do this. It felt like the right thing to do. You still got growing up to do and I want to make sure you have a fighting chance. Your dad would never admit it, but I know he was thankful he had someone to talk to when he got out of jail. I know he was happy I stuck around. Even when he was wandering the nights, calling it soul searching. I took him in to knock some sense into him. Even when he thought he would be a bad father, I pushed him to be better. To choose a better life for himself."

"You didn't stay long enough. You didn't stay for me." I swallow. "You didn't help him when he was raising me." I shake my head.

"He disappeared."

"That's an excuse! Everybody makes excuses." A tear slides down my face. "Where were you to stop him from letting his anger out on me and my mom? Where were you to stop the shouting matches, the belittlement, and mental abuse on me?"

Uncle Roger looks down at the item in his hands. A black cylinder.

"You don't know what Lasher's been through," Olivia says. "You don't know what type of man Harvey became. If you really helped him, he would've been a better man. He would've been a better dad."

"He might've even been alive today," Uncle Roger whispers. He licks his lips. "No one should put a hand on another person. No one should physically or mentally hurt someone intentionally. I'm not condoning his actions. Abuse is never an answer."

"I'm not him. I'm not your second chance." I feel another tear sliding down my cheek. "My whole life I've been trying to be this person . . . the person my dad needed me to be. The person that could take a hit. The person that listened. The person that was emotionless. The person that didn't question and just believed everything would work out. But, I'm not that person." I look at Uncle Roger. "I'm me, and I don't even know what that means." I sniff and wipe my face. "I'm useless."

"No," Olivia's dad says. He comes over and puts a hand on my shoulder. "That's not true."

I move away from him and walk around the table, in front of the TV.

"You're a survivor," Olivia says. "We're just teenagers, Lash. We're not supposed to know who we are yet."

"Harvey sent me a letter one year," Uncle Roger interrupts. "Saying he figured out fatherhood and sent me a picture of you and him. Pearly white crooked teeth y'all both had. Same parts on y'all head." He holds his eye contact on me. "He thanked me for sticking by him. He truly looked different in that photo. I called him and wrote back, but he didn't respond. I went to visit, and the landlord said y'all moved. No forwarding address. I believed Harvey was finally on the right track. I looked at that picture again, and I looked at how your eyes shone. Not for Harvey, but for the world. I laughed because I didn't know why a kid your age looked so excited. Like you were told you were about to go to the greatest place on earth. No, like you discovered it."

Uncle Roger shakes his head. "That face reminded me of Harvey's brother. Tim, was always going to bring something into this world. Do something for others." He sighs. "And he did, but . . . They weren't surrounded by enough love, by enough hope, by enough people on their side. I don't want you to be your dad. I don't want you to become me. I want you to be able to become you and know who that is. I just want you to do it with love around you. Lasher, you deserve to smile again like you did in that picture. To have hope again." Uncle Roger taps at the round item in his hand. He puts it on the table. "I got his ashes."

Olivia gasps.

I fall to my knees in front of the table. *His body was burnt?* He's in an urn. I grab it. That means his funeral was a closed casket?

"I'm sorry, Lasher. I truly am. I want to help if you'll let me." He pulls out something from his pocket, unfolds it, and holds it out across the table for me.

I take it and it's the photo of my dad and me. The one he said my dad sent to him. I look about ten or eleven in the picture. I suck in a breath. I put the photo down and slide the urn to the edge of the table. I stare at it. At him contained. I'm not him. Tears stream down my face. I do want family around. This is a day I've been waiting for, secretly. To meet others in my family and feel normal. I don't want to push everyone away. I want to be able to keep people in my life. I want to be a good friend. I want to stay in touch with the people I care about. I want to know what my dad was like before he was angry.

I bite down on my lip and look at Uncle Roger. "Do you promise to be honest when I ask about him?"

Uncle Roger sits up. "Yes." He nods.

I sniff and look at Olivia. I then look at the photo of my dad and me. I nod. "Okay," I whisper.

Chapter 21: Harvey
1989 – FALL

I was in jail for three months accused of running a red light, possession of a razor knife, and assaulting and battering an officer. It took another three months for me to have my second hearing after I pleaded not guilty. Mom and Uncle Roger found a decent lawyer. Uncle Roger told me the lawyer and them sought out any evidence they could find. The location where Tim and I were pulled over was caught on a store camera. It took two days for Ma to convince the lady to let us use it as evidence and that she'd be helping her two innocent sons.

The video has no audio, but shows that Tim never attacked nor put a hand on the second officer. It shows how the officer shoved Tim while he was handcuffed. Tim fell against the front hood and light. The way he fell, his head bounced off the front of the car and then banged to the ground. Watching it, I can't believe it happened to my brother.

The video shows some unnecessary roughness between the first officer and me. The charges of possession of a razor knife as well as assaulting an officer were dropped. But I still had to pay a ticket for charges of running a red light. The first cop still has his job, while the second one received paid leave. Unbelievable.

The night I got out of jail, Uncle Roger had me stay with him. He fixed me chicken, broccoli, and a sweet potato. He offered me a beer, but I don't drink.

So, Uncle Roger rolled me a blunt. We barely talked. The only thing I could ask him was about Tim. He said I'd see for myself tomorrow, but that he's less audible and thinner. A skeleton of the brother I knew.

I wondered was I a skeleton of the person I once was before jail? I got in one fight before laying low. My lawyer said I had to avoid incidents so they wouldn't mark up a reason to keep me in jail. I had to remember my goal to get out and see Tim.

. . .

Now, I'm at the house. My home. Where I belong. The couches and chairs in the living room are the same. The carpet reminding me of my childhood. The swinging kitchen door that held so many conversations behind it. But Ma doesn't want me here. I can't live with them anymore, she said. Uncle Roger said I could stay with him. It's bullshit.

Tim and I sit in the living room, Dad's chair supports his body best compared to the couch. We eat ham sandwiches with some orange juice. The weight and muscle he had just started to grow is lost. Tim's got memory loss of that awful day, but not of our upbringing.

"You alright?" Tim's voice is raspy.

I nod, swallowing my bite. "Yeah. Better now that I get to see you."

Tim smiles, the bone structure of his cheeks scaring me. "Ever . . . ever imagined me . . . sitting here?"

I shake my head. "Nah. I forbade you as a kid. Now, you just definitely don't belong there."

His smile drops, and he looks down at his plate. He's wearing a bath robe, which doesn't help the situation. It makes him look ill. He's got old gray sweatpants on and a sweatshirt with a sloth on it.

I chew silently. A chill goes through my sweater, and I don't think it's from the brisk air outside. This all feels weird, unreal.

"How . . ." he takes a long pause. He looks at the floor, not at me. "How did we become weaker than him?"

"What do you mean?" I scoot closer to him.

Tim looks at me.

"You alright," I ask him.

He nods and takes a bite of the sandwich not finishing his thought.

"Mom been spoiling you, cooking your favorites this whole time?"

He smiles, and it again scares me. But he doesn't respond.

"Has anyone visited you? From school or my friends?"

Tim nods but doesn't say who.

"Okay. Good, good. Glad people showed up." I chew. The silence between us unfamiliar. I'm used to us cracking jokes, or him asking for something, or just us sharing about our days. "Jail time was no joke. Felt lonely. But, uh, don't laugh." I scoot to the edge of the couch to lean closer to him. "To keep sane, I made up stories about people in my head. Like, what their life looked like before they were put in jail."

Tim just eats.

"I-I even made up what my life could've looked like if Dad and Ma split ages ago."

Tim looks at me now. "Mom blames him for everything now. She didn't used to be this adamant about it."

"I mean look at—"

Tim cuts me off. "You blame him for everything."

I swallow.

"I . . . I never saw it as his fault," he finishes.

"You got the best heart out of us. That's why, Tim."

He shakes his head. "The worlds messed up. You and mom should be blaming the way the world is ran."

"They chose to have us. They had responsibility. Ma held up her part . . ."

Tim has tears in his eyes. "We all had dreams."

I touch his leg. "Tim . . ."

"I had dreams. You had dreams. Mom had dreams. Dad had dreams . . ."

I'm silent.

"We all had dreams," he repeats.

I let go of his leg. "You're right."

He slides the orange juice out of the pocket it's been resting in between him and the chair. He chugs it down. "I want to lay down, now."

Uncle Roger said Tim's social energy drains in the afternoon, and he takes long naps. So, I follow him to the bedroom so he can lay down. I sit by Tim's feet once he's in bed. "I'm sorry it took me so long to see you."

Tim's eyes are wider with bags forming underneath them. He puts the covers over himself and holds a blank stare at me. He touches my hand though and it takes me back to when we were kids. This room. I used to help him not be afraid of the dark. Not hear Ma and Dad arguing. Not doubt school would make a difference for his life. I just used to . . . raise him. But my bed's gone now. Tim's got a queen bed to be as comfortable as he can. The walls look foreign. Now, I don't know how to help him. "You need me to get you anything?"

Tim shakes his head. He closes his eyes for a moment, then opens them again.

Ma walks in with Uncle Roger. "Time to leave," she announces.

"Elaina, he's your son," Uncle Roger says.

She goes on the right side of the bed, touching Tim's sheets. "Harvey's had his time. I don't want him to stay." Her eyes are only on Tim's face and pillow.

The words leave her mouth and I clench my fist. "How can you say that, Ma?" I carefully let Tim's hand touch the sheets and stand to look at her.

"Please go." She glances over her shoulder, but down. Not daring to look at me.

"Look at me, Ma!"

"St–Stop!" Tim shouts with a stutter. "No. No." He starts repeating it, eyes closed, shaking his head, begging.

Ma touches Tim's shoulder and starts to rub it. "It's okay, Tim. We'll stop. See we've stopped."

I start to get back on the bed, but Uncle Roger stops me with a hand on my chest. I look him up and down and he does one short shake of his head. "I'm sorry, Tim. We're not gonna fight around you," I assure my brother.

Tim swallows and opens his eyes. He looks at us. He lets out a breath and closes them again, before a tear could fully form in his right eye.

Ma grabs Tim's hand and rubs it.

"Come on, Harvey." Uncle Roger grabs my arm.

I yank out of his grasp. "Get off of me." I look at Ma and whisper, "You really gonna be like this to me?" I puff my chest. "Fine. I'll see you, Tim. I will."

Ma continues to look down at her hands holding onto Tim's carefully.

"He's my family. I took care of him just like you when he was growing up."

"You've grown up," she whispers. "It's time you leave. I'm trying to help you," her voice breaks. She puts Tim's hand to her lips to stop her cry from escaping.

"You don't have a right to cut me off," I still say. But I walk out and Uncle Roger follows. I pack my stuff.

Chapter 22: Lasher
2012 - WINTER

In court, I have to testify against Terry Warren. Bald Guy. And Jordan Flix. Long-haired Guy. I sit in black pants that are too big for me. Uncle Roger let me borrow a belt. I'm wearing a gray buttoned-up shirt to tuck in. I tried to get any other color but gray, but Ms. Lyn said that's all she could find for me. You can see my sweat stains in gray. I try to avoid it.

I'm on the stand, and I see people on the other side of the bench. Behind the wood barrier. Olivia's sitting there in gray dress pants and a tannish blouse with a white cardigan. Her dad is behind her. Her lawyer sits beside her. Uncle Roger sits behind them. I feel like I'm in a bad TV show court scene. These random extras don't want to be here. The sad part is my show wouldn't even be a comedy. As much as I love them, my show is an unfortunate drama. Tragedy? With no lesson. Just the perspective of a damaged teen boy.

I finally respond to the question of what happened on the night of December 22nd, 2011. "They kidnapped us . . . Terry and Jordan. They were looking for my dad, Harvey Patts."

"And did you let them know where your dad was?" my lawyer, Tom Walls asks.

He's one of those tall lawyer guys with short blonde hair. He always has one hand in his pocket.

"No. I didn't know where he was. He had left three nights before. But sent a text the previous day saying he would be home that night, which was the day Olivia and I were kidnapped. I thought it meant he had found a way to get money or a job."

"When you told Terry Warren and Jordan Flix that you didn't know where your dad was, what did they do?"

"They didn't believe me. They had us handcuffed to radiators in a basement. I told them I didn't know anything and neither did Olivia. They wouldn't listen. Terry was mad."

"Why?"

"Because my dad . . . he got with Terry's sister or something. He took Terry and Jordan's money." I shake my head. "I knew my dad would turn to betting; I just wish he didn't. But hearing what he did, it made me believe my dad actually had found a plan in a messed-up way. He believed he was going to win, so in that moment, I did, too. I wanted to." I swallow and look at Uncle Roger. I wonder how he feels hearing all this. What will go through his head as my answers continue?

"Then, what happened?"

"Terry didn't believe my dad would have the money. He punched me for looking like him."

"Objection."

"Overruled."

"Can you publicly identify who you're saying punched you?" my lawyer says, getting close to the stand.

I point to Terry, who has furred eyebrows, a sling holding his one arm, while his other arms rests on his lap. He's wearing a black button-up shirt and black dress pants. He's got two of the top buttons undone like he's some mobster.

"He even hit Olivia," I continue. "Jordan Flix threatened to shoot us." I point to Jordan before Tom could ask me to identify him, too. "He put a gun to my head. He said we didn't have to be alive for my dad to be taught a lesson. He threatened us."

"Even when you told him you didn't know where your dad was and just wanted to be let go, he not only kept you hostage, but threatened to kill you?"

I nod.

"To note, my client is nodding his head," Tom says.

I rub my hands on my lap. It feels too showy up here. Like I'm on a stage. My hands are getting sweaty. I try to rub the moisture off on these pants. "The basement was cold."

"How long were you in the basement for?"

"Two nights."

"Did they ever say they would release you?"

"No." I tilt my head to the side. "Maybe, when they got my dad. But it was also clear they might kill us as a lesson for my dad taking their money." I look at the judge who's nodding and listening to me. I look at the people and their blank faces. "It didn't appear they had a plan to release us. They didn't even feed us." *Do they care? Do they feel sorry for me? Or do they just want this over with so they can have their case handled?*

I'm mad that my dad left without warning, which led to this. Why couldn't I go with him? We could've dipped together. Then no one would've been at the apartment for them to kidnap. My anger causes my voice to rise. "They went a whole day without checking on us."

"When they did come back to check on you, what happened?"

I swallow. "It was the morning after the second night. My, uh . . ." He couldn't even look at me. He must have felt shame. He never shows shame. He got the money back. But, if our lives weren't on the line would he have left me or took longer to try to get the money back himself?

"Lasher?"

I blink. I had been staring right at my lawyer, but I had forgotten he asked me a question. "My dad was there. They . . . I don't know if they found him, or he found us. But, when my dad walked down the steps, he was beaten up. His shirt was bloody and ripped. And both Terry and Jordan had guns." I stick my fingers out, shaking, and point at both of them. I let my pinky finger and the finger next to it curl into my hand; and press my middle finger and index finger together and point them at Terry and Jordan. I let my thumbs stick out to the side. But then I lift my fingers straight. No longer sideways, my thumbs turn upwards. I'm pointing finger guns at them. "One at me, one at my dad."

"You–You are holding up your fingers in the form of guns. Are you mimicking the way they held the guns at you and your dad?"

My mouth hangs open, but I blur Terry and Jordan out and look at my fingers. I don't know. I pull them back and drop my arms on my lap. I sit up straighter.

"Jordan had a gun to the back of my dad's head. Terry had one pointing at my chest." I say it to Uncle Roger. He looks back at me, his eyes distant and serious.

"Then what happened?"

I turn to Tom. "Terry told Jordan to shoot me, but my dad threw his body back into Jordan and the shot hit Terry instead."

"Objection," Jordan's lawyer calls. He's got brown hair and is stocky. "That's speculative. How does he know my client was going to shoot him?"

"The gun was aimed at me!" I shout.

"You said Terry had the gun aimed at you," Jordan's lawyer yells. "Now how—"

"Wait!" The judge shouts with a hand up. His other hand lets the gavel hit the block. "Control yourself, Al, before I have to remove you." The judge then turns to me. "Lasher, wait. I speak first to determine whether you answer or not. Okay?"

"Yes." I look at him and give a nod. "Sorry."

"I will let the question stand. Answer, Lasher."

"The gun was aimed at me. He raised it from my dad to point it at me. Maybe my shoulder or head." I look at Jordan, and he's looking at me with dead eyes, lips pressed like he's trying to read my mind. His hair is tucked behind his ears, looking unwashed and poorly brushed. But one strand is in his face, and it makes him look more stone cold.

"So, you're saying both Jordan and Terry had guns pointing at you?" Tom interrupts.

"Yes. At first, he was teasing the gun back and forth between Olivia and I, like it was some game."

"Who is he?" my lawyer interrupts again.

"Terry," I spit out. I sit back. "Sorry," I try to adjust my body to calm down. There's no comfort in this small wooden chair. "But he, Terry, stopped on me. He held the gun at me. But, still told Jordan to shoot me instead. My dad interfered with Jordan's aim, and I didn't get hit. Terry got hit.

"Terry's gun flew out his hand and I tried to kick it away from him, but he got it back. My dad and Jordan were wrestling but Terry took over. He got up and pointed the gun at my dad. I guess he was mad he got shot and didn't care about killing us before my dad."

"What happened after Terry approached your dad?"

I suck in my lips. The shots ring in my ear, one after the other. "He shot my dad. Two times. My dad looked at me and said . . . said he was sorry. He looked at Olivia, and I don't know what he said"— Tears build in my eyes. *I'm sorry I couldn't help you, dad.*—"because I was crying, and then he shot him and shot him . . . dead." I look at the wood part of the stand, the divider between me and the jury, the lawyers, the defense. *You were crying dad. You said you were sorry. You said you loved me for the first time in three years. You knew you were going to die. That's what you were always running from. Not doing enough before you died. I wish you didn't go like that.*

I look at Terry and state the fact. "Terry Warren killed my dad."

"I'm sorry that you had to see that," is all my lawyer says.

I turn back to my lawyer.

"Did Terry or Jordan attempt to shoot you again?"

I shake my head once. "They didn't have a chance to. The cops came. I guess . . . my dad? He had to have told them, right?"

"That's a possibility."

"He was prepared to die. He at least had a plan for me."

My lawyer is silent.

"He gets to stop running. He gets to stop fighting so hard to accomplish everything. He doesn't have to try so hard anymore."

Silence fills the room for a moment and I only stare at Olivia's face. She has a tear in her eye and looks apologetic.

Chapter 23: Harvey
1994 - SUMMER

His arm droops around her as he caresses her arm. She rests in the crook of his underarm and her hand plays with the creeses on his pants. It's a night in for the both of them.

She breaks the silence and asks, "You seriously think you needed college?"

He rests his chin on her hair and thinks about it. He has always felt like he was missing out on life due to circumstances out of his control. He felt there was a normal way of living, which meant graduating elementary school, middle school, high school, and college. Then work, family gatherings or holidays, apartment living with roommates, then a house and becoming an adult on a path kind of mapped out.

When he looks at his path now, it's crooked. It's less family togetherness, less time making memories and mistakes with friends and no time for adventure. His life feels like desperation for a map or a button to place him back into a structure.

He lifts his chin off her head and says, "Yeah. I think you got something I didn't."

She turns to him. Her eyes close to a black, but he can see the beautiful dark chocolate brown color still come out. "How so?"

"I sometimes don't feel a part of society," he admits.

Her lips go to the side. "That's a bad thing? You're a writer. Isn't it good to be different? Aren't those stories valid too?"

Aren't those stories valid too? When he was a teenager, he thought his story mattered because he was on the path to high school graduation and college. He wanted to share stories of educated Black guys. He believed it mattered.

His path now, is no longer that. He feels like a disappointment. To never do anything that warranted jailtime, but still fail. But what if he was meant to share stories about experiences in life that don't look like the norm or stereotypes? What if his life is a norm too? What if someone did relate to his life? Could he fathom the parts of society that no book or movie yet discussed?

. . .

I've been in Pennsylvania for two years now, and I finally got my own studio apartment. No more living with roommates. I may be twenty-five, but I'm trying to embrace better late than never. I'm sitting on the couch with my girlfriend, Ariana. We've been together for a year and a couple of months.

"Your brother calls you HP, I want in on the nickname," she says. Her hand rests on my knee. Her nails are a light pink with glitter on them.

I have my arm around her, and she's asking me with her eyes to let her call me HP. "I don't know. Aren't you supposed to think of a cute name for me yourself? You are my girlfriend."

"You're not a sweetie pie, love bug, baby."

"You're babe to me. Cheeky," I whisper in her ear. "My cupcake when you're being sweet."

She shakes her head and moves back. "I almost never hear you call me cupcake."

I chuckle. "I wonder why."

She slaps at my chest. "You're not funny."

"Think of a nickname, and I'll let you call me HP, too."

"Patts?" she says questionably.

"Ew, no." I can't help but laugh. "That's the best you got."

"I don't know." She turns to me. "I don't want to be corny and say Harv. Hmm." She raises her shoulders.

She's cute when she's thinking. I get to stare at her chunky nose, her eyes go to the side, and she licks her bottom lip a little. I like her natural brown complexion, no makeup. Though she likes a touch of it here and there.

"Grumpy?" She blurts out, laughing. Her fingers scrape my chest for a brief moment as she leans forward and then back to see my reaction.

I blink. Did she really say that? "How is that a good nickname? Grumpy? No one even likes him."

"Everyone likes all the dwarves. No matter their names and personalities."

"Are you serious? You think I'm grumpy?"

She shrugs. "I mean sometimes you are. I'm not wrong."

I shake my head and remove my arm from around her.

"You're the writer, I'm not good with names and stuff." She tries to backtrack now.

"Clearly. You're something else."

"All I'm saying is sometimes it seems you should've taken some of your brother's programs."

I stand up now. "Fuck you."

A year after mom pushed me out the house, Tim joined a youth program to work with boys to stay out of trouble. But he was also studying the law about a person's rights in America. He wanted to start a program teaching young children their rights.

He first was volunteering at schools or after school programs and talking for free, but an organization liked his message and gave him a paid position. He's doing well for himself and Ma.

"Look at you," she says. She extends her arm out. "You're heated now. All I wanted was to call you HP." She stands up. "But you"—she points at me—"You wanted me to choose a nickname for you."

"I thought you had some creativity in your body!"

She purses her lips and uses her index finger to push me so she can walk by me. "You are grumpy. I wasn't wrong."

"Stop it."

She stops and turns to me. "Grumpy."

I roll my tongue across the top of my teeth. "Ariana."

"Grumpy," she says with an attitude now.

I take a step toward her, my right hand curls into a fist. "Ariana."

"Raising your voice isn't going to make me stop, grumpy pants."

I take another step forward and grab her, shoving her against the wall that divides the kitchen.

"Shut up. Just shut the fuck up!" I'm breathing in her face.

Her eyes are wide, and she curls her hand around her stomach.

No. No. I look at my hands and then let her go. I walk to the left, grunting and then punch the living room wall. I didn't mean to shove her into the wall. I didn't mean to scare her or our baby. She's two months pregnant. I'm not trying to hurt them.

"I'm sorry." I raise my hands up. "I'm sorry."

"You hit me!" She's shaking a little. Her eyes look straight into mine with sadness, worry, questioning.

"I didn't hit you," I try to say calmly.

"You're right. You slammed me into the fucking wall." She's using her hands as she talks. "Does that sound any better?"

I sigh. "You came at me, and you wouldn't stop."

Her hand crosses her chest in a swipe motion as she says, "That doesn't mean you put your hands on me."

I nod and come closer to her again. "My intentions were to just grab your arms. To just hold you still. I didn't mean to shove you into the wall.

I'm not trying to hurt you or our baby." I reach to touch her shoulder gently and then her hair. Her aunt recently straightened it for her. She's never let me see her natural hair. She always straightens it or puts it in a scarf or bun until she gets it done. "I'm sorry. I am."

She folds her arms and nods. "Okay." She swallows and looks down. "I'm sorry for repeating grumpy, like a child. That was dumb."

I lean on the wall beside her and sigh. I hold out my hand for her to grab it, and she does carefully. I hold her hand and close my eyes. "I'm going to try to be less grumpy," I tell her.

I feel her eyes on me, but she says nothing. She moves our hands to her stomach. To our baby.

Chapter 24: Lasher
2012 - WINTER

Uncle Roger met with Ms. Lyn. Getting all the paperwork and approvals took a week and a half. By the time I am ready to move, Olivia has found a therapist and is already two sessions in. She started back to school this week. I am leaving on Thursday. Wow, tomorrow.

It's my last day at the Jameses. They ordered out, invited Olivia and her dad, Uncle Roger, and Ms. Lyn, who couldn't make it. Uncle Roger has been staying at a hotel that's been eating into his pocket, so he's ready for us to leave.

"Thank you again for having this dinner," Uncle Roger says. "I know we're in a weird situation and I appreciate you looking after Lasher."

"We tried," Mrs. James says.

"In the end though, we see this is best. For Lasher to be with blood. It should help him," Mr. James says.

Mrs. James sits beside me, and Mr. James beside her. They start talking to Barry and Uncle

Roger about school prices. A topic I don't want to listen in on.

I stare at Uncle Roger, diagonal to the left of me. He is blood. The first blood-related relative I've met. I'm excited and it feels weird to be curious about what he has to say about my dad. Before, I trained myself to ignore other's opinions of my dad because they didn't understand where he was coming from. But he knows my dad. Knew my dad. He has stories. He will tell me things I don't know.

I think a part of me is hoping I hear some good. To hear that my dad wasn't always angry and reserved and isolated. That he felt love before. I don't think he loved my mom. I don't know what they had, but I don't think it was love. He was fitting her on as a relationship. But family, you're born into. I hope he actually loved them. But then again, Uncle Roger said he and his brother weren't surrounded by enough love. What did my dad go through? What made him this way?

"You okay?" Olivia asks me.

I turn to her. She's sitting across from me at the end of the table, her dad to the right of her. "Yeah." I nod.

"I'm not," she says. "You're moving."

I chuckle. It's true. She's one of my best friends. I also put her in a circumstance I hope to never be in again. I hope this is my only low. This feels like rock bottom, and I don't want to be back here, feeling shame and blame. "If I don't like it there, you'll be the first house I run to."

She laughs, but I know she doesn't like that answer. She takes a bite of her chicken sandwich and looks back at me and smiles.

"I think I'll be okay," I assure her.

She nods. "Okay."

"Yeah," I say, dipping a fry into my barbecue sauce and eating it.

After dinner, Olivia and her dad start saying their goodbyes before it hits 10 p.m. Barry hugs me, patting my back. "Take care of yourself. Call us when you get there."

I pull back and nod. "Okay. I will." He's about to turn, but I use the back of my hand to tap at his arm. He looks at me again. "Uh, thank you for everything." I raise my shoulders. "I didn't deserve the kindness you gave me."

"Hey, you're a good kid, Lasher. You're not your dad and you're certainly not his mistakes. You deserve to be cared for." He hugs me again. "Give your uncle Roger a chance."

He pulls back this time and I nod to his words. He turns to shake hands with the adults, and I turn around to see Olivia standing near the empty desk, watching us.

"Well," she says, as I approach her.

"Yeah. I'm sorry," I tell her.

"You don't need to apologize anymore."

I hug her, resting my face against her hair. "You're my best friend."

She wraps her arms around me and squeezes me. "You're my best friend too. Call, okay?"

"I will."

"And if you feel yourself spiraling back down, remember what Ms. Lyn taught you. And write if that doesn't work." She looks at me as we're still embracing. "And if that doesn't work, call us. You're not alone."

I smile. "Okay."

"Okay."

I nod and let go. She pulls back and I shrug. She smiles this time.

"I hope he's good family," she says.

"I do too."

The next morning, Uncle Roger arrives at the Jameses at nine on the dot. I barely could sleep last night, just wondering what his house looks like, how far he lives from Elaina. Wondering if he's got pictures of my dad, wondering if I'll even like him and trust him.

My two suitcases, one filled mostly with comedy movies and clothes, the other filled with as much as I could take of my life in Pennsylvania, go in the trunk. And a backpack with my dad's urn, notebooks, and the shoebox stay with me upfront. I awkwardly hug the Jameses and thank them for taking me in. It's a group hug and it feels genuine, which eases my mind a little. Then we get in the car and head on our journey to Massachusetts. I look back at the Jameses as we pull off.

Uncle Roger and I are silent for a good ten minutes. I watch as we pass people waiting for the bus, parked cars that are abandoned, windows replaced with trash bags. We pass an empty park.

"You hungry?" he asks.

I turn to him. "Uh, yeah. Yeah." More nervous.

"We could do a drive-thru or sit somewhere. What do you feel like doing?"

I shrug. "I don't know. Doesn't matter," I say to the right side of his face.

He bobbles his head back and forth. "What do I have a taste for? Mmm, I'm thinking some type of breakfast sandwich. You like breakfast sandwiches?"

"Yeah."

"Yeah. I get sausage, egg and cheese on a poppy seed bagel. Something 'bout those tiny things that hit just right for me."

"Where do you get that from?"

He smirks and glances at me. "Ever heard of Appetizers?"

I shake my head. "No. I've never been."

"Yeah. They're only a Massachusetts chain. Don't let the name mislead you though. They sell breakfast, lunch, and dinner. Their breakfast window is short, but you don't want to miss it. Worth every bite."

"For breakfast sandwiches I usually get—"

"Your dad used to work there," he continues.

I swallow. "He did?"

"Yeah. He'd never admit it though. He had a problem with every job he worked at."

"How many jobs did he have?"

Uncle Roger half chuckles, half just does a wide grin. "He had a bunch. You work before all the stuff happen?"

"Just babysitting or walking dogs. He said to just focus on school and join something."

Uncle Roger's lips press together, and he nods.

I look out the window. *Should I have gotten a real job? What age did my dad start?* None of my friends at school had a job. The seniors had jobs. Maybe some juniors. But, did anyone in my grade? No. Maybe one had a camp job already.

"You join something, then?"

I turn to him. "What?"

"Like a club or sport or after school thing."

"Oh. Uh, the school newspaper. I was an editor freshman year. My English teacher thought I'd do really well."

Uncle Roger nods. "Nice. An editor. Would look good on your transcript."

Great. Thinking of transcripts already. I'm going back to school. A new school. I have to be the new kid and be two quarters behind. I'm going to graduate later than my class. Or I'll have to do summer school. But why am I complaining? Before . . . I wanted to be back in school. I wanted to be learning. Or did I just want to succeed to make my dad proud? Because I knew that was the only true thing he always wanted for me. School.

I don't even think he actually cared about my grades. Freshman year, during winter break he'd said, "I hope school doesn't annoy you. I hope it feels like a chance. Catholic school is an opportunity. Yeah, you got your friends to get you through the days. Some teachers you like more than others. Some classes you get, some you're just getting by. But remember what it all means. It's shaping who you are. For better or worse. Make it good if you can. Give yourself a chance." Give myself a chance. That was always weird. Usually, we should give others a chance or a book a chance before we just dismiss them or it.

But, give myself a chance. I don't think I knew how. At least, not the way he wanted it. I thought he just wanted me to do really well. To excel and be smart and not give up on myself. But, maybe he was saying to trust myself. To give myself freedom to explore. It feels so off because I just wanted his trust. I wanted him to trust me with his thoughts and emotions.

I just wanted us to have a bond. I didn't think about what I wanted. I didn't care who I was. As long as we were good. As long as we had each other's backs and he was smiling or at least at ease, then I felt at ease. Yeah, I was wrong.

"He always half-said things," I say.

I feel Uncle Roger glance at me. He clears his throat. "Yeah. You were always wondering what his next move was going to be? Or what he was thinking?"

"Always."

Uncle Roger nods. "He never let anyone in."

"No one?"

Uncle Roger shrugs. "I want to say his brother, but I feel not even him fully. He wanted more to protect his brother and Elaina." He shrugs. "I don't know if Harvey ever confided in anyone."

"My guess is therapy. Well, his anger management group. Me and Declan could never sit in on their meetings, but when I was a kid, I believed they had a bond that no one could understand but them. I hope he was real with them."

"I might've seen some of them at the funeral."

"My dad never went back. When we moved, he only reached out twice to say we settled. He didn't want me to stay in touch with Declan."

"Elaina gave your number to your friend."

I blink and turn to him. *It was Elaina that gave Declan my number? She met them?*

He stops behind a car at a red light and looks at me. "Lasher, I'm going to tell you about your dad, but that doesn't mean you'll understand him anymore than you do now. It also doesn't mean you won't still be angry at him. It'll just click some pieces. I want you to settle in your head, now, how you want to move forward. I know Ms. Lyn can't be your social worker anymore. But processing and staying better takes consistency. I already told Angie, my wife, to start looking for a therapist or for you to at least be in touch with the counselor at school. But, I want you to tell me what you need also."

A horn blows behind us and he presses on the gas to move us forward. "Okay?"

I nod, "Okay." But swallow.

Chapter 25: Harvey
1999 - WINTER

I'm hosting a Sunday night football party because the Eagles may have a chance. They won their wild card game. If they win this divisional, I'll be surprised. I'm already surprised they lasted this long in the season. Their start had me believe it was another doomed season, but then the wins kept rolling for them.

I don't want to be having this party, though. What thirty-year-old man doesn't want to watch football? Me, because Lasher gets in crying fits, and they last like an hour. He has like three of them a day. Ariana and I both get headaches from it. Plus, work has been draining us. It would be great to just sleep today. But Chris, a guy I occasionally smoke with, wouldn't stop pestering me to watch the game at my place.

That led Ariana to invite her friend, Kimmie, who brought her friend Rae. Rae has Eagles spirit and goes all out with her outfits. She gets heated about the games just because she is born and raised in Philadelphia. She has an Eagles sweatshirt on as her coat. When she takes it off, she reveals she's wearing a number 20, Dawkins' jersey. She has blue jeans with an Eagles belt on.

Leroy, a person from work, comes over and brings his brother, Art, who may be a couple years younger than us. Therefore, I'm not getting any rest today. But with other adults around, Lasher tends to not get in his fits. He is more observant of the adults and the situation.

Ariana puts the grilled cheese and turkey sandwich stacks onto the table. We got a soda bottle out mostly for Lasher and me. I'm letting Ariana drink because it's an event. I usually don't like her drinking because I don't want to kiss her and taste the alcohol. I also can't stand the lingering smell of it in the air.

"Alright, let's make this interesting. Let's put a bet on this game," Chris says.

"I don't do bets, so you can count me out," Ariana immediately says.

"I'm in. What we talking? Score, flags thrown, injuries, false starts? What are we calling?" Rae asks.

"Just the score, please," Art says with wide eyes at the possibilities that Rae listed.

Chris shakes his head, and he bites into a grilled cheese. "They're gonna lose. Cowboys vs us? There's a reason we don't like the Cowboys."

"Nope. They're gonna surprise you," Rae says. "I'm calling it 30–14 in Eagles favor."

At least they're making the night interesting by betting.

Kimmie chimes in, "If Rae says they're gonna win, I'll believe her. I don't follow the sport, but I'll play along. 30–10. Give the other team less points." She shrugs with a smirk, taking a sip of her white wine like she was saying a smart tactic.

"What do you think, Harvey?" Chris asks. "Eagles winning or losing?"

"I don't know," I say. "It'd be ironic for them to come this far just to come this far. Or, they may keep going up and surprise us all."

Lasher sits beside me on the couch and keeps tugging my shirt and pointing at the table. I lean forward and grab the chip bowl and look down at him. "Is this what you wanted?"

He nods and starts to reach in the bowl.

I pull it back. "I want you to ask for it. No more pointing."

"Can I have the chips please?" His voice soft but audible enough, because he knows I only give him two chances to ask clearly before he can't have it.

"Yes."

"That was the cutest thing," Rae says. "I'm a sucker for kids."

"Try raising one," I say.

"He's getting better," Ariana says, rubbing her hand along my arm as she comes around to grab herself a turkey sandwich. She goes to the counter window seat, that divides our kitchen and living room and sits there with Kimmie.

"Those Eagles are losing 44 to zip," Chris says.

"You're wrong for that one," Ariana says.

"Little faith I see," Art says. "I'm saying those birds are gonna make it a tie game and lose in overtime. 23–20."

"Oooh, I'd like a good game like that," Rae says. She joins the ladies at the counter.

"Who do you thinks going to win?" Leroy asks Lasher. He's sitting on the other side of him, taking up space with a plate sitting on the couch between him and Lasher.

Lasher shrugs and lets crumbs fall down his shirt and onto his lap.

"I think they're gonna lose," I finally say. "Uh, by 10."

"What's the score though?" Chris asks.

I let my arm rest along the couch. "I guess 20–10."

Leroy shakes his head. "I'm going to vote in Eagles favor. 17–16."

"We're not voting my friend. We're betting," Chris says. "And you're forgetting the Cowboys beat them the last game. There's no way. What are our wagers?"

"Five dollars," Kimmie says with a snicker.

"No, no," Chris whines. "I said make it interesting. At least twenty dollars. Huh?" He looks at me. He sits in our solo chair.

I shrug. "I don't know, man. Sure, twenty?" I look at Rae, Leroy, and Art.

Leroy nods. "I'll put that down."

"Yall are newbies, so yeah," Rae says.

"Okay," Art says.

"Twenty dollars it is," I say.

"The person with the closest score numbers wins the bet," Chris says.

"Here, I'll write down everyone's answers, so we don't forget," Ariana says. She grabs a piece of paper from our room and a pen off the table.

And we watch the game. The first quarter is going as expected. Cowboys get a touchdown, and the Eagles have zip. The ladies and Art are tipsy. Ariana and Kimmie are talking loud, yelling, and copying Chris and Rae when they comment on plays. Rae even starts singing the chant because she believes that'll help the Eagles get their plays in order.

By halftime, all the Eagles do is a kick, and the Cowboys get ten more points. In another hour Lasher should be going to bed, so we make sure he doesn't have any more food or drinks. He's sitting on the floor in front of his bedroom door switching between playing with those weird Furbies and coloring everything brown in a coloring book.

"Smoke break," Chris says.

That's just what I need. When we come back inside, the third quarter has already started. The game's going nowhere. It looks like we all just might be wrong about the score of this game.

"Who said this would be fun?" Leroy jokes. "I'd rather hear a customer talk my ear off about a problem I can't help with."

I chuckle. "I didn't even want to watch this. Chris was hype for this game and betting."

"I thought the Cowboys would make it a fun blowout. Jeez, look at both teams wins and losses this year. I guess their defense is doing something right, but damn. I want more scoring."

Kimmie shakes her head as she sits with Ariana on the couch where Lasher and I had been sitting previously. "Football isn't for me. But fútbol. Give me some soccer, and now you're talking."

"Ugh," Rae and Ariana say. "Don't get her started."

"I never got into it," Art says. "American football and golf are my two."

"Very different sports," I say. I'm sitting at the counter where the ladies had been sitting previously.

"They balance each other for me. That rush and that focus."

Ariana comes over to me. She wraps her arms around my shoulders and kisses my cheek. "You mind putting him to sleep this time?" Her breath's sweet wine scent causes me to scrunch my nose. "Please."

I pull her off me, so she steps back some. "Babe, your breath. Come on."

"It's not that bad."

"You know I don't like it." I spin the chair to turn to Lasher. "Lasher, clean up your stuff and go to the bathroom."

He closes his coloring book and then grabs his crayons to put in his room.

"You don't see me complaining about your smoke smell."

"I didn't know it bothered you."

"I love you, so it doesn't matter." She sits in the chair across from me.

Lasher comes back to grab his Furbies to put away.

"I can't stand the smell. I'm not just gonna ignore it because of love." I stand up. "I got Lasher, though. Does that show my love?"

She rolls her eyes.

We're all hype by the fourth quarter, because the score is 10–20. Both Art and I said a score with the number 20. Art was hoping the Eagles pushed in some more touchdowns, but it ends 10–20 and no one is more shocked than I am.

"No way. Bullshit," Rae says.

"How did you do that?" Kimmie asks.

My mouth is open, and I blink, looking at the score as the players shake hands with each other. I called it? No fucking way. Tim won't even believe this.

"No one bets their first time and hits it right on the nose," Chris says. He throws his twenty dollars at me. "I'm watching you, Harvey Patts."

"We all give him $20?" Kimmie asks.

"He won. He not only got the closest score, but he got thee score," Rae says. She gets up and holds out the twenty to me. "You brought bad luck to my team."

I can't help but smile as I take it. "I was just saying stuff."

"Congrats, Harvey. Thanks for having my brother and I over," Leroy says. He shakes my hand and slides the twenty into it.

"I'm not betting again. Close one," Art says to me. He hands me a twenty and then helps grab some dishes and put them in the sink. Then, he and Leroy leave.

Ariana smiles. "You too, Kimmie. Don't try to sneak out of it."

Kimmie goes into her purse and pulls out a twenty, which she leaves on the table. "Next time I'm following you and not betting at all."

Ariana rests her head against Kimmie's. "Had to learn the hard way, huh?"

"Next time we're all watching the real futbol." Kimmie stands. "You ready, Rae?"

Chris, Kimmie, and Rae file out as well. I get off the chairs in front of the counter and plop down next to Ariana on the couch. "Babe, do you get what just happened?"

She scoots away from me to the end of the couch, so I don't talk about her breath. "Yeah. You won."

"I didn't just win." I drop the bills next to Kimmie's twenty on the table. "Five twenties. I just got one hundred dollars because of a football game. One hundred bucks."

Ariana smiles. "That is good."

"Fucking sports betting." I grab the twenties and lie them neatly one after the other on top of each other.

Chapter 26: Lasher
2012 - WINTER

I've been at Arnold West High School for two weeks. There's no school bell here, no uniforms, no church. The weirdest part isn't the students or how the neighborhoods feel different. It's not that it's not a catholic school and it's not that it's big. The weirdest part was when Uncle Roger and his wife dropped me off. When they met with the principal and the counselor. When they explained that they were my guardians.

This is the first time I'm going to school without my dad. He's not dropping me off or going to discuss payment plans with the office. He's not going to go to a parent-teacher night. He's not here to tell me to go to the corny dances or check out one of the school plays because it's hilarious with friends. He's not gonna tell me how important it is for me to be here. But I know it's important.

. . .

There's ten minutes left in my Algebra 2 class.

The two people behind me are whispering about movies. "What about *Milk*?" the guy asks.

251

"*Milk*? Like the slogan, 'Got Milk?'" the other guy replies.

I chuckle at his comment.

"No, you idiot. *Milk*. You didn't see all those commercials back in the fall?"

"I don't know what you're talking about."

"Harvey. Harvey Milk."

I swallow at the name Harvey. They're talking about someone else. Nothing to do with my dad. Nothing to do with me. But then I see him. He's in a sitting position, but not on the couch or in a chair. He's on the floor in the basement. I hear my voice stupidly crying out the word "no" that day. I hear the shots and drop my pencil on my desk. I cover my ears and look down. I want to pull my hands away to not stand out in class, but I hear Olivia and Bald Guy screaming at the same time. I press my ear to my left shoulder. Ten, nine, eight– I see my dad mouth the words, "I'm sorry." The shot fires and then another.

"You good man?" I hear from behind me. It's "Got Milk?" guy's voice. "Yo?"

"What's going on?" Ms. Walter says, but her voice sounds like she's on the first floor and I'm on the third trying to hear her. "Lasher, go see Aaron. Can you do that?"

I pull at my hair and look down at my shirt. My elbows press harder into the desk as I squeeze my eyes tighter, trying to stop the flashes of his body.

"I'll go with him," someone offers.

That fucking basement. That fucking basement. I raise my hand to my cheek. I could do it to snap some sense into me. But my hand presses into my cheek instead of slapping it. I'm rubbing it, trying to hold it together.

"Lasher?" I feel a hand on my back, and my eyes pop open. I nearly choke on my exhale. I untangle my fingers from my hair and look to my left at Ms. Walter. "Lasher, Nathan is going to walk with you to Aaron's office."

I look around the classroom. A couple of kids are ignoring me, but the person in front of me is turned around looking right at me. So is the person in front of him and behind Ms. Walter on my left. To my right, there's a kid standing. I guess that's Nathan.

I slide my notebook off my desk and into my backpack. The pencil falls and rolls under the seat of the person in front of me.

"Don't worry about that," Ms. Walter's says.

But I want my pencil back. I've already disrupted class though, so I'd rather hurry out of here than get it.

I zip my bag and stand. Nathan heads to the door, and I put one of my straps over my shoulder and follow him. He walks beside me, saying nothing as we walk the hall. I notice the sound of our shoes, the muffled lessons behind doors, and the running sound of a vending machine. I try to convince myself, I'm okay.

Nathan knocks on the counselor's open door. He's typing on his keyboard, eyes skimming quickly along the screen.

The counselor's name is Aaron. He looks like a college student, wannabe rockstar, while at the same time the guy in high school that no one could read. He wears a lanyard around his neck like he's a gym teacher with no whistle and wears a polo shirt and jeans. His hair is a sandy brown. He has weirdly styled side bangs, curling inward to the edges of his eyebrows. It is an even weirder length in the back because it's this little extra amount of hair that he might as well just cut off to have short hair, but instead he wears it calmly. Like the style has been cool for years. He raises his hand at me and motions me to come in. He looks like the type of guy that wouldn't have that many friends in school. But he seems like the coolest adult around.

"Hey, Aaron. Uh, Lasher needs some time with you." Nathan points his thumb at me, and I step in, with my hands holding onto my backpack straps, keeping me centered.

Aaron looks from Nathan to me. "Thank you for walking with him. Lasher, you can have a seat. You want to stay too, Nathan?"

He shakes his head. "Nah, I'll head back." He bumps my shoulder lightly with his fist. "You okay?"

Something easy to say. A default question. He knows the answer, but he wants the reassurance so he can leave. So, he knows that he did his part. Not even in a bad way. It was nice of him to offer to help. I'm not upset with him, I'm upset with the situation. I nod, and he nods back before heading out.

I close the door, not wanting anyone to hear why I shut down like that. I sit down.

"Give me one second. I have to send out this email and then we can talk," Aaron says, making eye contact with me shortly.

"Okay," I mumble. I slide my backpack to the floor and put my hands between my legs, pulling at each of my fingers.

Two or so minutes go by, just the sound of each key being pressed, before he clicks his mouse and then pushes his keyboard aside. Rolling his chair closer to the desk, he gives me his full attention.

"What brings you here, Lasher?"

"I, uh . . ." I sit up. "I couldn't calm myself in class. I was rubbing my cheek, wanting to slap myself, but I didn't. I tried practicing what Ms. Lyn taught me. But when my eyes were closed . . . it wasn't working. I was just . . . feeling it all."

Aaron nods. "How are you feeling now?"

"I guess fine. Not as tense."

"Good. Maybe leaving the classroom and walking a little helped."

"Maybe."

"Why do you think closing your eyes and counting didn't work out?"

I swallow and look at my fingers. I shrug. "Kind of . . . the first time I tried using it here." I look back at him.

"Gotcha. Roger told me that you like writing things out."

I nod.

"When do you write?"

"Used to be during the day. I don't know. Before I go to bed. Or, when I can't sleep. After school, only sometimes in school."

"Why only sometimes in school?"

I shrug.

"Do you think someone will judge you or ask what you're writing?"

"Maybe."

He nods. "If writing works better for you, then maybe you can ask your teacher if you can step in the hallway and recollect yourself. Bring your backpack, so it's not known to everyone that you need that time to write out your emotions. Or, if I'm available, you can come here. Tell the teacher you need ten minutes."

I sigh. "I only write to him." I bite my lip, wondering if he'll judge me for not writing about my emotions. Not really.

"You mean your dad?" he leans back in his seat.

I nod. "I thought that's what Ms. Lyn wanted me to do. Get out all my emotions to him."

"Yes. She definitely wanted you to explore all your emotions and feelings toward your dad. To explore and process everything you've been through. But also, I want you to understand, that that's your notebook. It's your time to write anything that comes to mind. Not only specific to your dad. Anything that may be difficult that you're feeling or even happy moments you may experience."

I tug at my small coils. "What if . . . what if I don't know how to write about being happy?"

"Well, I want you to know that you're allowed and deserve to be happy. And you can embrace those moments without guilt. You can feel them and grieve while processing it all."

I swallow. He said I deserve to be happy. How can I be happy that everything had to happen this way? There couldn't have been another way to happiness?

"Writing can help you get things out without being guided. You don't try to guide it, you let it guide you. The bad, the ugly, smiles, laughter, confusion. I know that's different then what you'll learn when writing academic papers. But this type of writing is for you. Your notebook and you. It may feel like it's for your dad, but it's not. It's for you," he repeats. "That's not selfish. You need that thing that's yours. That helps you. You should proudly have a thing that is yours."

I stop tugging at my hair and think about what he's saying. My notebook is where my voice can be my own. Where no one controls me, but me.

"Does that make sense?"

I nod.

He slides his chair back and reaches down, opening his bottom drawer. "Since working here, I don't always have the time to write during the school day, but I've accumulated six notebooks over the past three years. I've written with some students, but mostly at the end of the school day or before it starts. Sometimes, I'll write after a tough meeting or when I had a good night at home. As humans, we think all the time. We need a place for our thoughts to go sometimes."

Two of the notebooks are spiral, like an everyday school notebook, like mine. But the other two are flimsy, paperback. One has a skyline design, while the other has a saying on it. *I control the thoughts that come to mind.* The last two are pocket size notebooks. He put them in a line on his desk.

"Yeah, this one." He slides the notebook with the saying on it forward to me. "The olive green and gray colors were just alright, but when I touched the words, it was bumpy. I could actually trace each letter. And that day, at that time, it made the words feel ten times more special and fitting for me."

I let my hand run along the words. It's a nice feeling. Not braille, but still standing out. "I control the thoughts that come to mind," I mumble.

"Yes, you do. Remember that," Aaron tells me.

I nod.

"You feeling calmer?"

"Yes." It's true.

"Want to have a five-minute writing session? I'll write, too. And if you're moved to, I encourage you to share what you wrote, whether that be a line or the whole page. Or, you can tell me 'no' and those words can be just for your eyes. It's your notebook, but if you ever feel moved to share with someone, let it come from you wanting to. Okay?"

"Okay," I say.

"I'll share if I'm moved to, too. Okay?"

"Sure. Okay. Can I borrow a pencil?"

"Yeah." He reaches to his cup of things to write with. Sharpies, whiteboard markers, pens, and pencils sit in it. He hands a pencil to me with an eraser cap that hasn't been too worn down yet. I take it.

He then goes on his computer to pull up a timer.

"Can it–Can it be ten minutes? And I don't want to see the countdown please."

"Okay. Sure. Thanks for letting me know." He turns his screen more toward the left so I can't see. "Ten minutes. I'm starting it now."

We sit there in silence. He opens one of the school notebooks, the green one, and flips to the halfway mark of the book. I pull out my notebook. I'm about halfway into mine, too. I ignore what I wrote this morning and start on the right page. I write the date and look and find the clock behind him on a small desk. 12:14 p.m. He doesn't have an analog clock. I write the time in the corner, too.

Write whatever I want. It doesn't have to be about you dad. Will your memory be lost if I don't write about you? If I ignore you? Well, not ignore you. Just not write to you. Maybe it'll be good to write about other things. because I'm your son your legacy lives on anyway, right? Yeah. I should make it a good one. Not for you, or not only for you, but for me. For me?

I write the question mark slowly. It feels weird to be writing for myself? To be wanting to do something not for the better of my dad and me or any situation, just for myself to feel good about it.

I want a good burger and fries right now. I want to try other soda flavors like cherry or peach. I've always wanted to but feared they would taste bad. That's what's coming to my head. Random, but true. I wonder if Olivia is okay. I wonder what Declan is doing. So, this is what it feels like to write your thoughts? I kind of like it better. I feel I'm rushing to get everything down. superfast but not fast enough. I wonder what Aaron is writing and if he will share. Will I share?

I look at Aaron, and he has his chin resting on his knuckles. He's looking to the left at his wall, thinking. The pen in his hand is rising up and down. I look back down at my page and let my pencil write.

What now?

For the remaining minutes, my pencil knows my thoughts and when the timer goes off, I realize the randomness doesn't seem that bad. My mind isn't that bad.

"I do feel like sharing," Aaron says once he stops the dinging timer. "Just a few lines." He then reads, "*We're not losing loved ones. Love lives on. But where does the pain go? Is that what dies? Not just their pain, but any pain or anybody associated with their pain. So, that what's left can be positivity living on.*" He looks at me and shrugs. "That stemmed from my relationship with my grandpa."

I wonder when he lost him. Or if his grandpa raised him. "It was good."

Aaron chuckles softly. "It's not good or bad. It's just . . . thoughts coming out. Don't want you to fear being critiqued or judged. This is meant to just share and exchange thoughts."

I look down at the last line I wrote. "*Maybe my mind has been waiting to unlock the real Lasher,*" I read out loud.

Aaron smiles. "Maybe."

Chapter 27: Harvey
2000 – SUMMER

Six months later, and I've been on a betting kick. Five months ago, my job did cuts, and I was one of them. But, I took it as my opportunity to beat the system and show them I don't need their jobs. I can make money by myself. If I can bet with a strategy, I can make the same amount of money I did for minimum wage. I bet with old coworkers; I sucked it up and went to bars for football games. I made some good bucks the first few weeks. Sometimes just guessing which team would win got me money. Other times, my numbers would be close enough that I'd take home some nice change. The Super Bowl was the best time. I made over $2,000.

When football season ended, I moved to basketball betting. I told Ariana I was making this work for us to stay afloat. But she kept telling me to have a plan B and C because gambling wasn't steady income. I told her to look at our bank account, our fridge stocked with food, and us not being late for three months straight with Lasher's daycare tuition. I was doing my part.

When baseball season rolled around, I started losing money, though. I knew there was a way for me to bring it back up. I had all my eggs in one basket, as they say, and that was the problem. I wasn't diversifying my money. So, I explored lottery tickets and card games. Those lottery tickets are a straight up rip-off. But those card games, and the strategy involved, is all I needed. Twenty-one is the luck of the hand, and my hand gets lucky twice a week. I play Rummy when I need nights away from home, and Spades is my daily game I'm working on. The shit-talking and all.

I'm bringing our two bags of laundry through the door. We wash at the laundry mat thanks to the washer and dryer in our building being broken for a month. I stop when I see Ariana on the couch with her face in her hands, crying. I quickly drop the bags and close the door. I sit beside her.

"What's wrong? What happened?"

She shakes her head and wipes her face with the back of her hand before looking at me. Snot is coming from her nose and her eyes droop with sadness. "I . . ." she swallows. "This . . ." she swallows a lump and tries to clear her throat. "Everything. Everything, Harvey."

"What?" I ask.

"We're cutting it close with rent. Don't have enough for the electric bill, credit card bill, and . . . there's the car payments." She shakes her head. "HP . . ." she pauses and takes my hand. Her hand is damp. She looks up at the ceiling and swallows. "I've been scared to tell you this."

Tell me what? "Say it," flies out my mouth. She better not have cheated on me. She better not have—

"It's not fair you go out all the time and I don't. I want a life, too, outside of this house and family."

"Betting is my job," I tell her.

"It's not a job." She throws my hand onto my lap. "It's a distraction. A hobby. You need to get a real job."

"Not this real job nonsense. I'm—"

She cuts me off. "You're just avoiding me. Avoiding us. Your family."

"I'm providing for—"

"You're impulsive! You haven't been doing well for over a month now."

"I'm learning the games. The money has been coming up again."

She shakes her head. "It isn't enough."

"Come on. I'm doing great for someone that doesn't have a job. We're making it work. Just give me a couple of weeks, and you'll see. I got a system. Better than this controlling system we're run by. I'm making my own way to the top."

"You're not even at the middle. Come on, Harvey. You're smart."

I turn from her and look at our TV. But I stare at her reflection on the black screen, and she looks down shaking her head.

"I'm gonna go out. By the time I pick up Lasher from daycare, I'm going to have more money, and I don't want to have this conversation again."

Except, I lost $300.

And after dinner Lasher was playing in his room and we realized he left his favorite figurine at school. He always plays with it at night, so to not have it throws off his routine. He started crying. Ariana and I tried comforting him, talking to him, and giving him another toy to play with, but nothing stopped him. We left him in his room and moved to the living room. We have been trying to wait it out for twenty minutes.

"We need help," Ariana says. She's pacing back and forth in front of the TV.

"No, we don't. We can do this ourselves." I'm sitting on the arm of the couch.

"He's screaming now! No, we can't. Daycare can only do so much. He won't make it to kindergarten if he keeps up with this sensitive behavior. We should move closer to your family. Tim, your ma. Or Uncle Roger?"

"Leave my family out of this. Your family isn't here helping, either!"

"My family is never here!" She turns to me with her arms spread open. "My parents are traveling. They barely check up on me. And my brother is teaching English abroad! My family is never here. That's the problem. But yours is!"

She goes to the phone and picks it up, but I shove her against the wall and slam the phone back down.

"Are you serious?" she yells.

Lasher comes to the door, sniffing.

Ariana pushes me by my shoulder and lifts the phone. She starts to dial, but I get behind Ariana, trying to pull the phone cord out of her hands.

"I'm not playing, Ariana." I get my hand on the phone for a second before she spins out of my grip. "Don't make me break the phone."

"Just use your gambling money to buy another one," she counters with clear sass in her voice. "Oh wait, you didn't make any tonight, did you?" she shouts.

"I'm gonna make it back! This year can look up for us!"

"HP, I'm tired," she groans. She then presses more numbers on the phone.

"I'm not talking to my family!" I snatch the phone from her while pushing her to the ground. I slam the phone down on the hook and pick it back up to slam it down again. I press the hang-up button, in case she did call someone. "I'm serious, Ariana. I can take care of this family."

Lasher starts screaming again.

Ariana looks down at the floor, and her shoulders start to shake. I hear her moans.

My grasp loosens on the phone. I'm not trying to hurt her. "I can take care of my family," I say softer.

She sniffs and turns to me. Her tears flow fast down her cheeks. "Do you love Tim?"

I blink. "What?"

"Your brother. Do you love him?"

"Yeah."

She swallows. "Your mother? Do you still love her?"

"Yes, she's my ma." I am hesitant to take a step forward. To help her up. I don't get these questions.

She wipes her left cheek. "What about your uncle?"

I raise my shoulders and shake my head. What is she getting at? "I love him," I rush out.

"Do you love Lasher?"

"He's my son," I answer.

"Do you love him?"

"Yes."

"What about me? Do you love me?"

"Why are you asking these questions?"

She shakes her head and stands up sniffling. She wipes her eyes. "Harvey, do you love me?"

"What type of question is that?"

"An easy one."

We stare at each other. I had forgot the phone was in my hand until I tried to curl my fingers. Lasher's whining has turned into crying. I love my family. I look back at her and nod.

But she wipes her face and looks down. "You say you care about Lasher and me as your family. But you don't love us. He gets like this because of the way you treat me."

I place the phone down. "What's this about?" I can't even process what she's saying because Lasher is still going off. I turn to him and shout. "Cut the noise! Crying is a distraction." I grab his arm and back him into the doorframe.

"No! Get your hands off of him," she screams, hitting me on my back. She throws my hand off Lasher and picks him up.

"Are you trying to say I'm a bad dad?" I ask.

She lets out a breath and whispers to Lasher, "It's okay. It's going to be okay. You don't have to worry. *Shhhh. Shhhh.*" She faces Lasher's room, while he looks at me. I let her keep *shh-ing* until his cries become whimpers, then gasps of catching his breath, then sniffles, then silence.

I come over and use my shirt to wipe his face. I then touch his head, and he looks up at me for a moment before resting back on Ariana's shoulder.

She turns to me. "You're a bad boyfriend." She shakes her head as a tear falls. "I had fell in love with you." She walks into Lasher's room and closes the door.

Chapter 28: Lasher
2012 - WINTER

Uncle Roger comes in the living room and sits down next to me. "Mind if I turn on the TV?"

"No," I tell him. I'm reading one of my dad's chapters from the book he was writing. I can't believe he wrote his life down like this. He dated each chapter. Sometimes he wrote back-to-back. Other times he took months or yearlong gaps. I finish reading a chapter and he ends it by saying,

It would suck to be like authors before, who didn't live long enough to see their work impact generations.

It's weird to read him being so passionate about something other than earning money or me and my future. It's also weird that my dad is writing this in the same chapter where he's losing money during basketball season. He was still writing then. Still going after his real passion.

"Did you read all his chapters?" I turn to Uncle Roger.

He stops flipping through channels. "I did," Uncle Roger says. He turns up the volume on the TV a little as he settles on a rerun of a sitcom.

Every time I read my dad's stuff, I have questions. Well, more the urge to just want to talk to him about what he wrote. "I read it and get excited wanting to talk with him about his childhood," I say aloud. "The stuff I didn't get to know. And then I remember I already know the ending of the story. He's dead, and I can't ask him anything."

Uncle Roger nods. "It's hard. It's always gonna be hard."

"I'm sorry. I want to talk about his book," I admit.

Uncle Roger takes a moment and then raises the remote and turns off the TV. He adjusts on the couch to face me. "Alright."

"It bothers me that even as a kid he was angry."

"Yeah. He carried it like his armor."

I stare at him, waiting for him to say more.

"What stood out to me in his chapters, was that he showed he was sad in his writing," Uncle Roger finally says. "There was a lot of sadness in there that I wish he let the people that cared about him see in real life."

"Do you know if he tried to publish this?"

"I know he used to submit parts of it. But when he moved to Pennsylvania, he left almost all of

them here. So, unless he rewrote the earlier chapters
. . . You know technology has advanced since he
was a teen. Companies are starting to accept things
online. I don't know if he got into typing his drafts
and then having the whole book on some
document."

I try to remember if I saw my dad ever
typing. We had a home computer at one point, but I
only played games on it. I really can't remember but,
he did keep writing. I have his last three notebooks.
Not many compared to when he was younger, but
still something.

"He wanted to make a difference like Tim,
Uncle Tim, did. He wanted to give young guys hope
through his writing."

"Gee, how far did you get?"

"I'm an okay reader. Fast when I want to be.
Slow when I want to be."

He does a soft laugh. Then starts to wiggle
his foot, as if to wake it up. "I don't know if his
book was hopeful, though."

"It's honest."

"What's the point in him writing all this? I
still don't get the point."

For some reason my head jerks back, and I
feel anger rush through my body with what he just
said. "He existed. That's the point."

He looks at me, surprised by my tone. He lets his knee rest on the couch and rubs his ankle. "I'm not saying Harvey's existence wasn't important. Far from that. Books have messages. Books—"

I cut him off. "Books are a journey."

"Indeed. But this is a lot. Some of it not necessary for a reader. I'm glad writing was his peace of mind. Lord knows he needed something to calm his head. To calm that anger. But, some works are just meant for the writer."

I nod, taking that in. Was this really my dad's diary in disguise as a book? If he had went to college, maybe that would've helped him write better. Write other things.

"Did Elaina ever read his work?"

"No. I don't think so. She just encouraged him to keep going because she knew it was his dream."

"What was your dream?"

"Me?" his mouth opens, partly a smile and partly puzzled.

"Yeah. Did you achieve your dream?"

"I had a family. I have a family," he corrects. "I promised my mom I'd always watch over my sister, and I kept that promise. I—"

"What about not related to family? Something you like or wanted."

"Well, when I was really young, I thought I wanted to be a police officer. Then I got older and thought I wanted to be a lawyer. Fast talking and trying to speak up for somebody. But by the time I got to be eighteen, I realized I wanted whatever allowed me to have a good paying job, to get a good house, to just be doing good. Not selling drugs, not being a mechanic . . . I'm no musician or artist. I got nothing against people that do what they gotta do to survive or make it, but I didn't want to have to struggle endlessly. But, my path was still tiresome. Long days. Slow days. I didn't really like working in the factory, so I moved to working at a market. Then that landed me an opportunity as a salesperson which changed my whole career from selling food products to selling people appliances."

"And that paid well?"

"Moving up did. And being with the right company. The key was also sticking with that company for a long time. I was there for years, and it definitely took longer than it should've, but after a few rejections and 'not yets,' I got my raise!"

"Did you like it?"

He shrugs. "I had moments. Met some good people. Had some reoccurring families. That made it nice. But, it's a tedious job at the end of the day. It did for me what I needed it to do. I'm thankful for what it provided for me and my family."

I nod and look around the living room. I see what he has because he took a more traditional life. In a way it looks easy. But it's not. It's a choice.

Chapter 29: Harvey
2004 - WINTER

At age thirty-five, I open a letter from Ma.

Your brother died on January 23rd, 2004. His funeral has already passed. I now realize how ignorant it was to not tell you about it. I was caring about my feelings when it was your brother's day. He would've wanted you there. He is buried at Chestnut Oak Cemetery in Massachusetts.

Harvey, you should know he asked me to forgive you. He asked you to forgive yourself. He asked me to forgive myself. But I can't. I regret too much.

The choices I've made . . . Sometimes, I think I just messed up when your father and I got in that accident. Other days, I know better and knew long ago the choice of staying with him was wrong. But I loved his past passion. I loved his potential. He talked of doing so much. He included me and made me feel loved for a while. But, by the time Tim was old enough to speak sentences, it was clear there was no love between us anymore. We were just choosing to stay anyway. Why? You wouldn't like the answer. You never did. I regret a lot of parts of my life with him. I know he regretted it, too. We wanted to achieve things that just didn't work out.

Harvey, I regret making you how you are now.

I regret all the times I stared in your eyes and knew what you wanted, and I never listened.

We failed as a family.

Your mom.

That's the closest 'I'm sorry' I'll get from her. Full of excuses. Of gaps. Half-explanations.

I throw the paper to the ground. I stand up and kick the table. I turn to the wall, thinking I'm going to punch it. Instead, I get closer and closer to it until my fist presses into the wall. I bow my head and rest it there, and tears fall from my eyes. Those anger management classes got to me. I can't bring myself to take it out on what's in front of me anymore.

My brother's gone. Tim's gone. What type of brother am I? What type of brother was I? We only texted here and there. I stopped trying to see him. I let my new responsibility be the only family I focused on.

What type of mother is she? Failed as a family? She pushed me away from my family.

. . .

That night, I'm sitting on the couch with a rolled up blunt in my hand and the TV on mute. I haven't lit it at all.

"I can't sleep," I hear Lasher say.

My son is nine years old. I wasn't good to his mom. Ariana left for good this time. One of our last screaming matches ended in an honest talk, though. It felt like we were in our twenties again.

"I'm done. I can't do this anymore," she shouts.

"I can do right by y'all," He shouts back.

"No." She takes a breath. She lowers her voice as she says, "I should've never settled. I thought it would be better to call a place a home rather than always traveling, never having a comfort place. But, I was wrong for thinking I could be better than my parents. I'd rather be alone and see the world, than be stuck and miss out on it."

He's silent. He takes in her words.

"We can take him to a foster home and then go our separate ways." The him she's referring to is their son.

He shakes his head. "No. I still believe I can be better than my dad."

"Harvey," she breathes out.

"I'm not ditching my family. That's what you want to do."

Her face tenses. "I'm doing what's right."

"So, am I! I'm raising my son. I won't lose him again to you and not to some strangers."

"You're impulsive and lash out!"

"I won't hurt him."

"You're pathetic!"

"Why? For loving my son?"

"For not accepting that you're not who's best for him!"

He feels the heat rise from his fist, up his arm, across his chest, and through his teeth. "Get out!"

"Gladly!" She stands. She throws open the door to reveal their son crouched in the hallway. He's not crying or whimpering, he's just sitting there, curled up, listening in on them.

She pauses for a second and stares at him before rushing by. She flings open the door and disappears. She leaves it open. But their son just sits there. He doesn't run after her, but his eyes stay fixed toward the open door.

. . .

I want to raise a Patts that succeeds.

I turn to Lasher, almost spacing him out completely. I blink and wipe a tear. He's standing there in his too small pajamas, rubbing his big sleepy eyes. His haircut's looking strange on him now, as he and I both had grown used to his fro. I put the blunt on the table and go over to him. "Nervous about presenting your project?"

Lasher nods.

I clear my throat. "You'll be alright."

"Is Mom gonna come back?"

I sigh and bend down. His mom has been gone for almost two years. "It's you and I, Lasher. She had to go. She had to . . ." I grab his arms but look at the floor. "I'm here." I swallow. "I'm gonna be better for the both of us." *I have to.* I stand back up. "Now, go on back to bed." I turn to the TV.

"Can you come back with me?" Lasher asks.

This question hits me in my gut. I whip back around. It wasn't Lasher who asked me that question, it was Tim. I swallow, knowing he will fall back to sleep if I'm there. I place a hand down onto his shoulder. "Yeah, Tim. Yeah." Lasher doesn't correct me.

He's my family.

Chapter 30: Lasher
2012 - WINTER

There's a ten-minute break, then two more classes before lunch. I go to the counselor's office. His door is open, a student is shooting a tiny ball into a hoop hung on the wall.

"I'm definitely going to get an A in his class, I'm just mad they put me with Doug." He makes it in the basket.

Aaron raises his hand at me and motions me to come in.

The boy turns around. "Oh hey. Want to shoot?" He may be a sophomore or junior.

He tosses the ball at me before I can respond, and I miss it. It bounces from my arm to the floor and out the door. I catch it before it rolls down the hall.

When I return, he says, "Sorry. I thought you'd want to shoot some hoops, too."

"No." I toss it back at him and he catches it with one hand. "No, I just wanted to . . ." I trail off. Talk to Aaron? Not be stuck in the hallway hearing people chatter about people I don't care about or know during the break.

Aaron looks at the boy.

"I should go grab something to snack on before my English quiz anyway. Thanks, Aaron." He puts the ball between some pencils in a pencil cup and then grabs his backpack that was on the floor leaning against Aaron's desk.

"See you, Cal," Aaron says.

Cal walks by me and out the door.

"Come in, Lasher. You can close the door."

I turn and do so and then sit across from him.

"How ya doing?"

I teeter my head. "I just wanted a break."

Aaron nods. "Yeah. That's understandable. Cal comes here when he wants to talk. He doesn't usually sit. He likes the ball. Helps him be able to do something with his hands while he talks."

I nod. "Didn't mean to interrupt."

"Oh no. You're fine." He leans back in his chair. "Every time you and I meet at the end of the day you seem exhausted. So, I'm actually glad you came by. I was wondering if you wanted to change our time?"

"No," I say quickly. I like that I get to leave my last period classes early. I feel I get to breathe. I've officially been here for a month and all my teachers know it's a requirement for me to go to the counselor because of my situation. Instead of feeling outcasted by it, I feel like I get the best end of the deal. "No, I'm fine with missing most of last period."

He nods. "But is it helpful?"

I nod.

He doesn't look convinced but doesn't question it. "Have you written today?"

"Yeah."

"Anything you want to share or talk about?"

I slide my backpack off and onto my lap. I unzip it and pull out the red notebook. I open to what I wrote yesterday. I skim past judging a girl in my class for giving three-minute responses to questions every time she speaks. I skip wondering what Olivia and Penny are doing in class right now back in Pennsylvania. I clear my throat and read,

"Sometimes, I'm here and it doesn't feel like I'm here. It just feels like I'm watching what's going on in the day. But, when I'm alone or back with Uncle Roger and Angie, that's when time moves again and I'm a part of what's going on."

I make eye contact with him.

He nods. "Thank you for sharing that. Adjusting to a new school can be hard."

I shrug.

"Once you find a friend or something you're interested in, that viewer perspective might stop, and you'll feel a part of the day."

"I don't mind it though."

He sits up and starts rolling a pen on his desk. His fingers look as long as the pen. "Well, that's good you're not frustrated by it, but I don't want you feeling isolated." He is looking at the pen.

"I don't."

"Hm, let me rephrase." He makes eye contact this time. "I don't want you to isolate yourself."

"I just don't know how to talk to anyone."

"Yet," he says.

I sigh and close my notebook, then put it back in my backpack.

"You didn't want to get any food during break?"

"I ate some cereal during Mr. Ether's class. EAT AND LEARN is his motto."

"Ah, yes. The coffee and snack king."

"He says he shares snacks if we get an A on his test."

"*Tsk tsk*. Bribery."

I smile. "He says jealous teachers that don't like his teaching style, call him Mr. Eater."

He smiles. "I'm not a teacher." He turns his chair. "But do you mind if I go grab a snack real quick?"

I'm thrown by him asking for my permission. I shake my head. "No. Is it fine if I hang here for a bit?"

"Okay." He stands. "I'll be back but leave when you're ready." He pats his pockets to make sure he has what he needs, then leaves, leaving the door open.

He comes back twenty-five minutes later. It's fifteen minutes into my next class. I was planning to not go to Spanish class anyway. She goes too fast. Not just when speaking, but right after the marker leaves the board, she calls on you to answer a question. She gives no room to process the new vocabulary. Like I'm supposed to suddenly know the meaning automatically? My mind doesn't work like that. I need more visuals. A slower pace. A teacher, not an assumer.

"You're still here?" He sounds out of breath. He returns to his seat munching on a pastry and holding an orange juice. "Using me as an excuse for missing class?"

"I thought you'd be back earlier."

"Did you work on homework at least?"

"No. But, I wrote a poem."

He sticks the last bite in his mouth. "Hmm." After he swallows, he asks, "When did you start writing poetry?"

I got into poetry last week.

"We're learning it in English class, and I like how easily poets can describe outdoors. They make you see the visual right in front of you. I want to get that way about my emotions. See what I'm feeling right in front of me."

He nods and sits back. He uses a napkin to wipe his mouth. "Want to share it with me?"

I pull out my blue notebook from English class. I don't want to share the poem I just wrote in his office; it's sad in a way. I've been thinking about my friends and how I don't have any here. I don't want him to try to have me talk about it. So instead, I'll share the poem I wrote in English class. I've been liking writing my own poetry. I did this besides starting our homework early for tomorrow in class. I like reading the poem for homework in my own space. To truly decipher and absorb it, so I'll be able to analyze what's being said without distractions.

"Okay," I tell him once I find the page. "It's about Spanish class. I was dreading having it today."

He sips his orange juice and nods for me to read.

Her voice like a buzzing bee

Fast and in my ear

When I shoo it away

The buzzing returns in my other ear

So I run away

Down squeaky halls and metal lockers

I end up at the counselor's office

Not for counseling

For silence

For discovery

For myself

The choice is mine

Mind

My mind

My thoughts

For anyone else to hear?

The answer that comes to mind

Both in Spanish and English

It means the same

No

He smiles. "I like it. You move from physical location to mental location."

"Huh. That's a deeper way of putting it," I say.

"How do you feel about it?"

I shrug. "Was just an escape. A moment."

"It's a good start."

"Thanks."

"Maybe you'll get into the literary magazine or the school newspaper."

"That's too much pressure."

"In what way?"

I shrug. "I'd be editing other people's work."

"Or submitting your own. You could also work on a specific section of the magazine or paper for layout or formatting. Don't you miss lit mag?"

"I just wanna get through school."

"Don't forget this is your new home. Find something that interests you. You have to think about college too."

I swallow. College. Huh. Surprisingly I don't feel panic or sadness at the mention of it. My dad is in my mind, but I don't feel sorry. I feel hopeful. "Uh, I just want to focus on one achievement at a time. No one . . . No one in my family, well my dad's family, ever graduated high school," I admit.

Aaron nods. "Oh. So, this will be a big achievement for you."

"Yeah. It's actually been an overwhelming thought, until now. Before, I'd spiral at this thought and conversation. And I'd want to ask my dad so many questions I didn't get to ask. But Uncle Roger told me why my dad's brother didn't graduate. Why my dad didn't graduate. I'm no longer left wondering. I still wanna do it for him. I want him to be proud. Well, really for the Patts to win." I bite my lip. "But I do want to graduate, too. Finish school and feel . . . normal?"

"You feel your family isn't normal?"

I shrug. "My life."

"Everyone's life looks different. There's no one way to live."

"You say that, but there's specific expectations and norms."

Aaron nods. "There are other kids that have been through trauma. There are other kids that have lost their parents. There are other kids that have gone through foster care. There are other kids that had to move away from the home they knew. It just happens to be that all that happened to you. What's normal is that life deals us challenges and obstacles."

"I just don't want to have this talk, Aaron!"

He nods. "Okay. I'll hold off for now."

"Thanks."

"I do want you to go to Spanish." He turns and looks at his clock. He sighs. "The twenty minutes you have left." He grabs a sticky note from out of his top drawer. "I'll write you a note. But, you can't just stay in my office if I'm not here. Okay? You need to keep up with all your classes. Not play anymore catch up."

I nod. "Okay."

"I'm going to walk you. You have Merta, right?"

I nod.

"It would be best if she has a written and physical presence from the adult."

"Thanks." I stand and slip my backpack onto my shoulders. I take the sticky note from him.

But what he said has got me thinking. Am I overthinking being normal and making myself less normal by hiding away at the counselor's office?

Chapter 31: Harvey
2011 - WINTER

At age forty-two, I pull out my cellphone. My whole life I've had an unhealthy relationship with my family. I thought having my own would change that. But it's still a mess. All I tried to do was keep my son in school. I can't even do that right. All I tried to do was be a better dad than mine. I'm tired of feeling this way. I'm tired of failing. I'm tired of letting someone down. I'm sick of trying to do better and ending up worse than where I started. There's no point anymore.

I sit sideways on the chair in front of the hotel desk, propping my left arm on the back part. My right hand holds my phone. I let out a breath as I press the buttons to dial Ma. I haven't spoken to her in nineteen years. But regardless, I'm still her family. This is the last thing I'll ask of her.

It rings once, then twice, then a third time. The fourth time, I think I'm going to have to leave a message that I'm praying she'll hear and call me back. But, to my surprise the ringing cuts off, and I hear, "Hello." She sounds tired. I look at the time, and it's 1 a.m. I've been going at it late every day for the past two months. I forgot to consider if she'd even be awake. But this is my only option. I've gotten myself into dangerous shit and dragged Lasher into it.

"Hi, Ma. It's me."

"Harvey." She says my name with a bit of perk instead of dread, agony, or worry. "It's been so long," she whispers.

"Hi, Ma." I repeat. "I uh, need a favor."

She's silent.

"Ma, I need 20k. I'm hoping you and Uncle Roger can get it by tomorrow. I know that's last minute, but it's for Lasher. Your grandson. He's in a dangerous situation that I got him mixed into. He's a good kid, Ma. He puts up with me. I don't want him ending up like a Patts. He's gonna graduate high school, Ma. He's gonna be whatever he wants to be and be happy. I can't give him that. He's bright like Tim, but I'm in his way. This is the last thing I can do for him. I don't know what you think of me anymore, but I stopped being mad at you. I had to. I'm hoping you'll do this for me."

She's still silent. No reaction. Nothing when I said the price. Not even a breath when I revealed her grandson's name. I forbade Uncle Roger from telling her, but who knows if he did anyway.

Then, sounding like she's talking through tears she says, "I'm sorry." She then sniffs.

My eyes widen, and I clench my left fist.

"I'm sorry you're in this predicament. I'm sorry I wasn't there for you."

I then realize, she's not turning down helping me; she's saying the apologies she never said before.

"I'm sorry I kicked you out. I'm sorry I blamed you. I'm sorry I didn't explain things to you. God, I'm sorry you didn't see Tim more. I'm sorry you weren't at his funeral."

Tears build in my eyes. I'm silent now. My head shakes, not wanting her to list them all.

"I'm sorry I never got to see my grandson as a baby. I'm sorry I didn't help. I'm sorry some of your anger was because of me. I'm so sorry, Harvey."

"It's ok, Ma," I whisper. I suck in a breath. "I'm sorry too."

"You have nothing to be sorry for."

I use my thumb to brush a tear sliding from my eye.

"We'll get you the money. Yes."

"Ma, I have to tell you—"

"No. No, let this be our moment. This here."

I look at the ceiling, shaking my head. Why did it have to take so long? Why did so many years have to pass to hear her voice again. "I missed you, Ma."

She sniffs. "You, too."

"I hope you meet Lasher."

"I will."

I swallow. "Thank you for doing this."

"We're family. We forgive no matter the extremes. It's what we do. You're forgiving me, and I'm honoring you." Her voice cracks, "We pull our weight to show our love. I'm taking care of you." She's weeping now. "Oh God."

"I wish I could hug you, Ma. It's going to be okay. This is what I needed. I love you."

"I," she gulps. "I . . . love . . . you . . . too."

I nod. "Ma, I gotta make another call. Okay?"

"Okay."

"Okay," I say.

She hangs up.

I blow out a breath like I've just taken a hit of weed. For a second, I think there could be another way, but I know there isn't. This is the right way to do things. So, I dial Terry. He picks up on the second ring. "I got the money."

I lift the bottom half of the phone away from my ear, press the top edge against the side of my head, and close my eyes. I did this. I did this to my life. I did this to my son. I suck in a breath and shake my head. I open my eyes and sit up.

No, Harvey, you fixed this one. You fixed this.

Chapter 32: Lasher
2012 - SPRING

I look at the clock and it's 2:10 a.m. Luckily, it's a Friday. No, wait. Fuck, it's Thursday. Why can't I sleep? I turn on my side and look at the wall across the room. I can see the outline of my desk. I close my eyes, but they reopen. This is my life now. Actually, I guess I always had restless nights. Worrying about my dad would keep me up for weeks sometimes.

This just feels different. I don't know what I'm worrying about. I used to think I wanted medicine for it. But, when Ms. Lyn suggested it, I turned it down. I feared I could slip into an easy addiction to sleeping pills. To antidepressant pills. To anything that can relieve my stress automatically. I know Declan used to take them when we were kids. Donnie was glad when he got him off them.

Ugh, I want to sleep. I can do this. Just close my eyes. Let out a deep breath. And zone out. Think about nothing. The silence. Hmm. Whew. Hmmm. Whew.

I open my eyes again. It's 2:17. Not thinking is not working. *Do I really want to get up? No. I want to sleep. Why tonight? Fine, I'll write.* I lean off my bed and reach under it for my new notebook. Aaron just gave me this one. Now I have my own notebook with a quote on it: *A thought could get lost unwritten.* I don't really like it compared to his. But, it does have the bumps where I can feel each letter. And I'm sure Aaron didn't just choose it because it was the only one like this. Well, I hope he didn't. That would be cheap. Not even trying to have it speak to me. But hey, it was a gift, nonetheless. I was surprised, so can't complain too much.

I sit up and let my feet touch the cold floor. I walk across my bed, around my desk chair, over to my desk and hit the light on. I grab a pen and a pencil just in case the pen runs out. It's been needing the scribble technique too much recently. I walk back to my bed and sit on it, moving my pillow against the wall to rest against it.

I open the notebook to the first page. Clean and clear, a blank lined page. It's always weird starting a new notebook. In classes I feel rushed to have to start writing. But, here, alone . . . It's like why do I have to start?

Because I want to go to bed, I remind myself. *Okay, okay.* I scribble in the top right corner on the other side of the fading pink line. It seems the pen will work. What to write?

I can't sleep. That's why I'm writing.

Yeah, it's true. But, what else do I want to say. Maybe I just want to read. I could read a poem instead of writing. Have some deep poem put me to sleep. Or maybe I could read my old stuff? I haven't done that before. That would be different.

Maybe that's why I can't sleep. It feels so weird to see how I am now, compared to then. Like two different mes. I reach under my bed again for my last notebook. I just finished the last page this afternoon. That's why I'm finally using Aaron's gift weeks later.

I open the red notebook, skimming past the first three or four pages, before opening it completely to remind myself of my thoughts back then. But I had forgotten they weren't my thoughts. They were my letters. My confessions. My link to the afterlife. Thinking about it now, it was like a darker version of writing to Santa. Letter to someone who you'll never see, not because they're not real, but because they're dead.

Hi Dad,

I wanted to let you know I lied to you every time you told me "you got this" and to trust you. I never trusted you. I wanted to. I tried to force myself to. But, I was always just scared. Worried for you. For us. I was mad at you. And I know I just told you how mad I was yesterday, so I'm not going to say it again, but dad...how could you not see it? Over and over again asking me to trust you. You shouldn't have to ask. A parent shouldn't have to ask. You should've already had it from me, but you didn't. And no, you weren't like before. I know that. I know you're better than that version of you. Or...you were better than that old version of you. But, then you were a new bad. You just still needed help. Ms. Lyn is helping me. I'm not gonna push away help anymore. I can't if you want me to graduate.

But, see I said that just to make you feel better. I always want you to be okay. That will never change. Or, I guess it will since you're dead.

Is this just a pathetic letter? Nonsense? I just wanted an honest conversation. We were always bad at those. I'm still bad at those.

I forgot how I sounded in those letters. I don't want to think about them, so I flip to later on. But of course, I land on another letter I actually remember writing. I was crying while writing this one. It was when I kept testing the Jameses, and I thought they'd get rid of me and that I'd truly be alone. That I'd have no one. Look at me now. I'm with Uncle Roger and his wife. I'm living with actual family. I'm getting comfortable in this house. I haven't talked to my grandma yet, but she wants to meet with me. She wants to see me face-to-face. Maybe that's why I'm so anxious. This is real. I can't believe I'm here. I can't believe what's happened. Four months of true speed. How is it May?

I look down, surprised to see my phone's screen light up. Olivia is calling. I open my phone and look at the time. 2:48 a.m. "Hey," I answer.

"Oh my gosh, hi," she says. Her voice is soft, but she sounds surprised to hear me.

"You're still not sleeping?" I ask. The last time Olivia and I talked was three months ago or so, and she seemed to be struggling with sleeping and socializing.

"No. But, I at least sleep twice a week at night." Her speech is rushed. "And I take naps now, during the day, to help get used to sleeping again. It's actually been working." Man, I hate that she's struggling.

"I, uh, I'm having the opposite problem. I don't nap, and I've been sleeping well."

"Oh. Then why are you up? Did I wake you?" Her voice now frantic and apologetic.

"No, no. Some nights are still hard. They just come randomly. Tonight, was one of those nights."

"Do you have flashbacks when you close your eyes? Or hear the gunshots?"

"Not when I sleep. But at random times in the day, yeah."

"Oh. Then. . . what did you mean . . . by some nights are hard?"

"Life. Being here. Me, in Massachusetts. That this is real. That, I'm okay. We're okay." I wince because she's not okay. "Safe," I try to clarify. "I feel like my mind is still in disbelief of how natural this adjustment is coming for me. It's weird."

She's silent.

I slide my notebook off my lap and swing my feet off the bed. Should I not have said that? She did call me.

"So, you're adjusting well?" she says softer. Sadder.

I swallow. "Yeah."

"I miss you," she says.

"I miss you too, Olivia."

"I can't stand school," she says.

"I try to avoid it," I say.

"How?"

"I meet with the counselor before the end of school every other day. But, he's chill, and I sometimes hide out there during lunch and even skip classes to do work in his office or just write. I don't know. It helps me get through the day."

"That wouldn't work for me. I really can't stand talking to Sister Margaret."

"What about your therapist?"

"I mean . . . yeah. Yeah, but I don't see her every day," she says. She then let's out a gurgle like chuckle. "Today she told me to reach out to you again. I'm glad. Though, I don't think she wanted me to do it at this time of night."

I chuckle a little. She does, too. "I'm sorry I haven't reached out," I tell her.

She's silent. This time I don't wait for her to speak again.

"Massachusetts happened so fast. Processing it all is happening so slow. I felt there was never time to just stop. Days keep going and going and going. And some days, it feels like I'm a guest just getting to watch Uncle Roger and his wife, Angie's, life. Except, they're also taking care of me. They don't expect much of me besides going to school and trying. Just keeping my grades up. They clearly have it together and don't need me . . . to help. Instead, they're helping me. It feels so fake. But I don't want the mirage to end."

"You're getting to see how it would feel to have both parents."

I swallow. I never thought about it like that. A household I could've grown up in. What parental figures could look like. What they could be.

"I should have reached out more, too," she admits.

"That's okay. You're processing things, too."

"Yeah, but . . . I want to be a good friend. I'm trying to keep my friends. Lately, it's been hard to communicate." I wonder if that means she's not even talking to Penny.

I nod. "Yeah. How is Penny and your friend, Chuck, doing?"

"Good. Penny extended our friend group. I could get along with them if I tried. Chuck is excited to graduate. He's still got my back." She sighs. "I don't know. I don't really hangout with them. I'm attempting to through movies."

"A good choice. What movie?"

"Just old funny ones. I don't want to go to the movie theaters."

"Fair." I hesitate, but ask anyway, "Is it darkness in general that still creeps you out?"

"Yeah. Yeah."

"I'm sorry, Olivia."

"I sleep with the lights on and make it work."

I nod. "To calm myself I write."

"That's good. I color. Use coloring books or sheets. Keeping in the lines calms me."

"Nice. I think school is harder for me than living with Uncle Roger. My grades are just okay. C's and like one B. I did get a D I'm trying to bring up to a C by finals. Making new friends and all that is just . . . different. I miss you and people I know." I pull at my hair. "But a good that's come out of it is that my counselor helped me not write to my dad anymore."

"Nice," she says.

"It's more random. Now, I write about my thoughts. About school. About the day."

"That's good."

"Want to hear one?"

"Really? Yeah, actually."

"I've also gotten into poetry, so—"

"Poetry?" she says, surprised. "Really?"

"Yes. It's interesting to me."

"Boring," she interjects.

"It's chill."

"Alright, alright. Sorry. I was just caught off guard."

"And try not to judge my writing too hard, okay?"

"I won't," she says. "I won't." She reassures me.

"Okay." I let out a breath and flip through my notebook to newer stuff. I land on a really raw piece. I want to skip it, but reading the first three lines, I know it's right. It's important, and I need to not run away from it. "Okay," I say again and start reading it to her.

Me.

Lasher.

I'm capable and I mean it.

I'm lovable and I mean it.

I matter.

And I can't believe I mean it.

I can't believe I almost chose to die

Over myself

Over life.

I let out a shaky breath.

Over a future I could have.

My heart is racing a little. I can't believe I'm reading this aloud.

I'm thankful.

And I didn't know what or who to thank

before.

And now I have thank you's to give

And the first person that deserves to hear these words

Is me.

Thank you, Lasher.

For what? That's what I'd ask myself.

And the answer is . . .

For

Feeling.

"Wow," she says. "Yeah, that was . . . real. That was showing another side of you, Lash. I can't believe you wrote that."

"Me neither. My heart is still racing from just reading it to you."

"I'm glad you shared it with me. It wasn't boring or cringy."

I smile. "Cool. I think I'm realizing how much I talk to myself, and it's weird."

She giggles. "We all talk to ourselves. We listen to our own thoughts."

"You know what I mean. I hear my thoughts, I write my thoughts, I think some more. I'm always thinking."

"Have you made any friends?"

"No."

"Well, my therapist had me make a goal for myself to communicate with the friends I have and get better at standing up for myself. So, maybe your counselor can help you make goals for yourself."

"I don't know."

"That's what he's there for. Ask him. Then, you have me to report back to as default, so you're not always in your head."

I smile. "Okay. Sure, I'll figure out what my goals should be."

I can tell she's smiling when she says, "I'm glad we talked."

"Same. I uh, I have some news."

"Yeah?" she asks.

"I'm . . . I'm gonna meet my grandma. I'm meeting Elaina."

"Wow," she says.

We talk for another half an hour. I tell her about people in my classes and then we go over our subjects that overlap. She fills me in on some school drama and then how her and her dad's relationship is going.

. . .

It's Tuesday, 4:30 p.m. I'm at Elaina's house with Angie. She understands how big of a step this is, so she's waiting in the car while we meet.

I'm holding a pot of my dad's ashes. I'm giving her some of my dad because he was her son. She helped him help Olivia and me.

I stand in front of the brown door, just staring at it. I've been here for two minutes. All I have to do is knock. When was the last time she saw my dad? Would she have even recognized him as an adult? That's a stupid question, she probably saw his body before it was burnt.

I take a deep breath and let my finger press the doorbell. It's an *annnn* type of sound that comes out.

I hear an unlocking and then another. She has a peephole, so she must have already seen me. I take another deep breath. The door opens, and I freeze. Her hair is wrapped in a scarf. She's wearing a long brown cardigan over a flower-patterned shirt and purple sweatpants. She sucks in her bottom lip. Her hand touches her mouth. Her other hand holds onto the doorknob.

"Hi," comes out my mouth, barely audible, like I'm catching my breath.

Her eyes squint in awe. "Hi, Lasher." She clears her throat. "I'm sorry we didn't meet sooner." She comes closer and wraps her arms around me.

I step into her hug and my left arm wraps around her. She smells like cherries and cinnamon. My right arm cradles my dad's ashes like a football. In a way, it's like a three-way hug.

An embrace that's been long overdue.

Thank you for reading! Reviews helps others add a book to their shelf. If you enjoyed this book, please consider leaving a review on the site you purchased from.

HOME ~~SWEET~~ HOME Discussion Questions

1. In Chapter 1 Harvey's mom says, "You pull your weight to show your love" (p.2). Can you name a few scenes in the novel that show characters demonstrating this expression?

2. In Chapter 5 the reader learns that Harvey writes down events that happen in his day. How do you process different events that occur in your day? Do you prefer to write or engage in a different outlet to process?

3. Consider Bald Guy and Long-haired Guy's choices in Chapter 10. What do you think would have happened if the cops never arrived? And how would this effect Lasher and Olivia differently?

4. Why do you think the author chose this story to be both about Harvey and Lasher, and not just Harvey alone?

5. Anger appears to be a theme throughout the book. Both Harvey and Lasher feel anger for different reasons. What have you found helps you when you are angry?

6. In Chapter 7 and Chapter 21 the reader is shown how contrasting Tim and Harvey's relationships were with their dad. What impact do we see their dad had on them? Are there any similarities?

7. Lasher says, "In a way it looks easy. But it's not, it's a choice" (p. 280). What is a recent choice you made that looked easy to an outsider, but was difficult for you to choose?

8. Do you think Lasher's notebook entries and poems show the reader another side of him? What information helps the reader decide?

9. In Chapter 16, Lasher says, "If I failed due to choices [my dad] made, then I had someone to blame. But, if I failed without him, then . . . I'm no better than him. I want to be better than him" (p.153). In Chapter 29 Harvey says, "No, I still believe I can be better than my dad" (p.284). How does the title connect to the goal they seek?

This guide has been written and provided by Desirae Moten for classroom, library, and reading group usage. It may be reproduced or excerpted for these purposes.

**Another book by Desirae Moten,
Stay-at-Home Calls for Poetry**

"my voice within is emerging. it's time I *inhale,
exhale, release.*"